# VELVET AND STEEL

*By the same author*

The Vineyard Inheritance
A Handful of Seeds

# VELVET AND STEEL

*Elizabeth Daish*

ROBERT HALE · LONDON

© Elizabeth Daish 2002
First published in Great Britain 2002

ISBN 0 7090 7085 3

Robert Hale Limited
Clerkenwell House
Clerkenwell Green
London EC1R 0HT

The right of Elizabeth Daish to be identified as
author of this work has been asserted by her
in accordance with the Copyright, Design and
Patents Act 1988.

2 4 6 8 10 9 7 5 3 1

Typeset by
Derek Doyle & Associates, Liverpool.
Printed in Great Britain by
St Edmundsbury Press, Bury St Edmunds, Suffolk.
Bound by Woolnough Bookbinders Limited.

# VELVET AND STEEL

# I

'Come close to the fire. You look as cold as a stone!' Lady Hester Clinton felt the chill from the damp cloak that the girl slipped from her shoulders, and watched her stretch out her hands towards the blazing logs.

'Thank you, my lady,' said Hope Levett. 'It's a long road from Lichfield in this weather and after all the tales I heard from my brother, I was frightened. He says there are beggars and cutpurses and worse, and a girl must be careful to avoid trouble.'

'John or your father should have set you on the road and given you a nag to ride,' said Lady Hester. She also put her hands closer to the blaze as though the girl had brought more than a chill with her. 'It isn't safe to walk all this way alone. Did you meet anyone on the way?'

'A coach passed me and several mounted men who looked from their habits to be of Cromwell's band.' Hope shivered. 'I hid in the bushes each time I heard hooves, and then I got caught up in the brambles and nearly screamed, thinking I was being attacked.'

'It must be all of four miles from Lichfield, and rough going on the old Salt Road,' Lady Hester asserted. 'We are nearly into Alrewas and that road is no place for a female alone. I shall speak to your brother when I see him.'

'John wanted me to take the nag, but I shan't be going home again until later in February or March and he'll need it, and my father doesn't like me working here. He thinks I might get tired of the walk if I do it often enough and so go back to tend house for him.' Hope smiled, faintly.' It was good of you to let me go home so soon after Christmas when you had so many visitors at the manor.' She looked at her mistress with gratitude. Who among the great ladies of the county, and even in the whole country, would be as good to her maid as Lady Hester? Who would have her into the big hall and let her warm herself at the fire?

'Your mother was my maid and a friend. I was fond of her, so why not you? You work hard and have a gentle hand with lace. I find Sam Levett more surly each time I see him, as if I have done a disservice by taking you into the manor.'

'It reminds him that my mother served you and, I think, grew to despise him. That's why he jibbed at me coming here,' said Hope. 'But I couldn't stay at home any longer. He gets worse and worse, and only John seems to make him see any sense. I just make him mad and he frightens me.'

'You are your mother's reflection as I remember her,' said Lady Hester. She glanced at the slender fingers and delicate wrists of the girl, and at the graceful curve of her neck under the thick dark hair, and realized with a shock that Hope was not just pretty: she had a kind of unselfconscious pride that owed nothing to the heavy features and slow mind of Sam Levett, her father.

Hope sighed. 'There are other matters that eat into him, my lady. Two men were hanged for poaching last month and that stuck in his craw. He makes no secret of his belief that all game should be free for all and that hanging is a sin when it's for stealing a hare or a doe.'

Lady Hester laughed. 'The man's a fool. He's a commoner in charge of the cathedral's game and fish ponds, and yet he talks like a poacher. It is the law of the land, and right too. How may we protect our own without punishment for felony? Thank the good Lord that we are not troubled here too much by the Puritans, who would stop all hunting and cockfighting and other manly sports, and make our lords and masters kick their heels and turn more to wenching!'

'I am warm now, madam. I came back a day early as I know that there is much to do here and you have guests. John shod some horses that were taking a coach to Alrewas, and three other gentlemen put up for a night at the inn, so I thought they might be coming this way, too.'

'I'm glad you're here. Dorcas is useless when it comes to dressing my hair, and her fingers are thick, coarse and hot. I shall rest for an hour. Come to my room with a tisane before I dress for supper, and press my lilac silk with the velvet pinner and the pale blue petticoat with the roses.'

Hope picked up her cloak. 'Yes, my lady.'

'Go first and change your shoes. Your feet are soaking, girl. Then ask Abigail to give you a draught of sack to warm you, and tell her to warm ale ready for the gentlemen when they come in from the field.'

Hope went quickly to her room under the eaves of the huge and ancient manor house that had seen summer follow winter for more years than Hope could imagine, and tore off her thick stockings and shoes, changing them for fresh dry ones. She hurried down to the kitchen and found Abigail basting a fat doe as it turned on the spit over a tray of root vegetables. Hope stood holding her skirt hem towards the fire to dry off the last dampness and Abbie filled a mug with hot spiced ale and gave it to her, before heaving her enormous bulk on to a stool and drinking from a quart pewter pot that was now nearly empty. Her face was crimson from the heat of the fire and the fumes of the spiced ale, and her eyes sparkled as if the world were a very pleasant place through the mist of ale.

'You came back early. What, no lad to tumble you in this cold weather?' Her heavy shoulders shook with laughter.

'There's enough to do here for my lady,' said Hope.

'Did you walk all that way? You missed the mail and one lost a wheel, they says, and stranded six people in the mud far from any hearth.' Abbie looked secretive. 'They say they were spies travelling from Oliver's camps, and the wheel came off with a little help! It's time they settled this nonsense for good and all. What's wrong with His Majesty? He goes to church like a God-fearing man should and was chosen by Heaven to rule. It's a wonder that Cromwell and his crowd don't get struck down by thunderbolts.'

'My father thinks we need a change,' said Hope. 'He rants about fornication and over-indulgence, and tried to make me read terrible pamphlets against the King.'

Abbie adjusted her neckcloth and wiped her face with one end of it. 'Sam Levett is a fool,' she replied in a slurred voice. 'He was ever a fool and can't see further than the end of his nose.'

'Many men think as he does, and some might say they do if they feel that Cromwell is coming too close for comfort. His men have taken many towns and even now, in 1643, when we thought it would all be over, his men roam the country, taking what they want and leaving death behind them. Even the King has no rest. He stays at Oxford with the court, or so John said, and Parliament lords it in London where Cromwell forces his laws on the people.'

Abbie looked sly. 'Does John, your brother, feel as Sam does?'

'John hates no man,' said Hope, simply. 'He tries not to side with anyone and yet I know he favours the King.'

'So the son isn't like his father?' said Abbie.

'Nor is the daughter!' asserted Hope, tossing her hair back from her face.

'The daughter?' Abigail's attempt at bland innocence became a leer. 'What daughter?'

Hope looked confused. She had seen Abbie in her cups often enough during the four months since she came to work at the manor, but now she was swaying as if she might fall. 'If you drink any more, you'll never have supper ready for the company,' said Hope.

'The company?' Abbie blinked and staggered over to baste the meat again. 'Such company,' she said, and laughed. 'Four old friends of the master and one fine foreign gentleman that will make every woman in the house want to raise her skirts for him. Made my toes curl just to see him in the hall,' she added.

'Even you, Abbie?' said Hope, laughing.

'Why *not* me, you slut?' Her mood was changing. 'You may

have blood in your pretty veins that Sam Levett never gave you, but there's many a tune played on a big fat fiddle like me!'

'What do you mean?'

'What everyone knows but you. Your grandmother was taken the night before her marriage by the lord of the manor in the village where she lived in those days. They call it the right of the lord . . . in French, the *seigneur*, or something. First flower to him and then free to go to her husband. That's why your mother was a fine lady in all but name. Blood tells.'

'But that was my grandmother, Abbie. My mother married Sam Levett and there was no such custom here, or none that I heard of.' She was smiling. Abbie was fuddled again, but suddenly what she had said made Hope falter and lose all sense of mirth. 'Sam Levett is my father. If that had happened, it would have been John. He's the first born.'

'Your mother worked here and was with child long after John was born. Some say that Sam never took her to bed after John was born, and some said she refused him and ran away to her service here. Happen you was a miracle birth, and happen there was a nice young man staying here with eyes for a pretty face and a lust fit for the king himself . . .

'You are drunk! It isn't true! It can't be true.' Hope sat down on a bench stool and remembered words said in anger at home; harsh words and blows and names that made Hope want to shut out the remembered sounds of 'slut' and 'wanton' and 'cursed of God', while her mother wept softly and grew paler and more silent and faded into a decline before she died.

There was a night when Sam Levett came to her room after

too much drink, and groped for her body through the bedclothes that she tried to keep up to her chin. She had screamed and had John picked him off her as if dismissing a puppy, his broad shoulders and muscular farrier's hands gentle in their strength but his face more angry than Hope had ever seen it. His slow power made Sam know that if he ever touched Hope again, there would be no gentle restraint, but bloody murder so, at sixteen, Hope had gone to work at the manor.

'Go to her ladyship, but don't dream that you are like her,' said Abbie. 'Find a nice lad from Lichfield and get married.' She finished her ale and belched. 'Keep away from the great hall and the men, and come and help me clear after supper. I think I have an ague and my eyes are cloudy.'

'The pressing!' Hope exclaimed, and fled. The linen closet was already set up with a wide table covered with layers of cloth and two flat irons sat on the hob of a small range. Hope filled a bowl with water and found a piece of thin clean linen to put between the iron and the rich silk to avoid iron mould stains and other marks that could ruin the fabric. Gradually, she forgot Abbie and Sam and everything but her interest in the work at hand. The sheen of the lilac silk and the frills of lace that fluted out under the iron made her hold her breath and wonder at the beauty of the gown. The velvet pinner she hung over the steam of a kettle to bring up the nap, and she powdered the silk slippers and brushed away the slight stains, making them almost as new.

She hung the gown over the airing rack and finished the petticoat, then held the dress against her own body, turning this way and that and making the taffeta sigh. Abruptly, she put it down. Sam had been angry when she wore the gown she now had on, cut down from one of Lady Hester's but still of good fabric and showing no sign of wear. The deep mauve colour made her skin take on the soft lustre of a pearl and her eyes appear deep and glistening as the violets soon to bloom in the hedgerows. She looked far too much like her mother for his comfort.

This dress is fine, but I must never think that I am dressed like Lady Hester, she told herself firmly, but her hands lingered on the cool fabric as she took it along to the boudoir before making the tisane and waking her mistress.

The hangings of the canopied bed were drawn back and the room was warm. Hope stirred the fire and made a blaze. Lady Hester sighed. 'I wish I had more female company,' she said, as Hope helped her into a robe. 'Tonight, I shall sit with six men who talk of nothing but the chase and politics. If my son were here, it might be different, but I shall not see him again for another year.'

'Has Mr Charles written, my lady?'

'Often, but it does nothing to lessen the pain I feel at his absence. My husband insisted on him taking a year or so on the tour in Europe, and seemed in a hurry to get him away before he volunteered for Prince Rupert. If I had daughters I would be content,' she said, and watched the face above hers in the huge gilded mirror as Hope frowned in concentration while she brushed the pale hair into elaborate curls. She thought back to Isabella, Hope's mother, and wished that she had been more courageous when Hope was born and Sam Levett wanted the baby farmed out to whoever would take the brat that he swore was not from his bedding. If I had adopted her then, she thought, there would have been scandal as people would have said she was begotten by my own husband, forgetting that he had been away for over a year dancing attendance on the King, coming home briefly at infrequent intervals.

She smiled as Hope pinned a silk flower into a swathe of hair. 'You are right. It looks softer than jewels,' she said. There had been a moment when she had wondered if it was possible that Edwin, her husband, had taken his fill of the maid, but as Hope grew there was nothing of Sam Levett in her face and nothing of the Clinton chin or eyes, and Isabella's lips were firmly shut to question, and remained so until her death.

'You look beautiful, my lady,' Hope announced at last with real pleasure at the result of her handiwork. 'Such lovely hair that is easy to dress, and the sapphires bring out the colour of your eyes.'

For a moment, the older woman took Hope's hand and put it to her cheek. 'I am grateful, my dear. You make this old place a brighter and happier home, and I want you closer to me when Sir Edwin is away. Make up the bed in the room across the way and find things to furnish it as you will. There are chests and stools enough in the attic doing nothing but gather dust and the worm. You are more than a lady's maid; you are my companion now. You must still do my hair and all the duties you have now,' she added, hastily, 'but I shall pay you an extra five pounds a year and give you more comforts and clothes.'

'My lady!' The sudden colour and sparkling eyes told Hester all she needed to know.

'Say nothing to the servants,' Hester suggested. 'The room

can wait for a week until these gentlemen have gone, and Dorcas would be upset if she knew that I gave you preferment. You shall drive with me into Lichfield whenever I go there and so need not stay in Quonians Lane with your family unless you want to do so.'

'Take Dorcas the next time you go,' Hope said, and smiled. 'She hates travelling by coach and dislikes the people in Lichfield shops, so she might then be glad to think you take me to save her the trouble!'

Hester laughed. 'You are a minx! I shall go when the roads are bad and be far too busy to see that she is fed well. Dorcas would rather gossip in the kitchen with Abigail than step outside into the air.'

'I told Abigail to have mulled ale ready, my lady, and I heard hooves and men's voices. I could go down and tell them in the kitchen that the gentlemen have arrived.' Hope wondered if Abbie was still on her feet and if the other kitchen maids had enough initiative to cover her lapse.

'Yes, go down and send Dorcas to the Great Hall with the ale. They will drink before they change their clothes and shed the mire. We shall eat in an hour. When our guests from Alrewas arrive, Dorcas can bring them here for sack or Malmsey wine before supper.'

'So you will have some female company, my lady,' Hope consoled her. 'The two ladies from Alrewas will brighten your evening.'

Lady Hester made a very unladylike moue. 'We shall play at cards and my cousin cheats,' she said cheerfully. 'No music, no play and no good conversation. I yearn for London or Oxford, but it is not safe to ride in a good carriage and wear silk or velvet in the city now that Oliver's sombre fustian dresses the town. He shuts theatres and ale houses and forbids church services if they seem too high. Edwin advised me to keep away from the court as tongues wag and there is no way of knowing who will come out of this conflict the loser. He is faithful to His Majesty but says there is no need to run into trouble, and gentlewomen have been insulted by Oliver's crude Roundheads.'

'I could help Dorcas take the ale,' suggested Hope.

'No!' Her reply was vehement, and Hope regarded her with surprise. 'I want you here,' Hester said in a more controlled voice. 'The men will want to be easy, to talk and swear and drink their fill, and they take no heed of Dorcas.'

Hope flushed. 'I am no wanton, madam.'

'No, you are not. You are as pretty as a picture and I feel I must look to your future as if you were my own,' Lady Hester said, ruefully. 'You will not go near the men while they are too . . . relaxed, or until you dress as my companion, when they will show you respect.'

Hope called for a chambermaid to see to the fire and to tidy the boudoir, and went down the narrow back stairs to the kitchen. Abigail was snoring by the fire and one side of the roast was darkening as the spit grew sluggish under the inept hand of the scullery maid. Bread lay fragrant and hot under a cloth and the dish of turnips and carrots was ready. Soup simmered gently in a huge black pot and the fowl were dressed and kept warm. Hope breathed a sigh of relief. Most of the preparation had been done before Abbie began to drink and there was little harm done as Dorcas had mulled more ale and was ready with a huge pewter tray, mugs and a white cloth.

The woman looked sulky when she saw who had come into

the kitchen, but Hope smiled and said, 'Lady Hester wants you to see to the men, Dorcas.' She wrinkled her nose as if annoyed. 'I have more pressing to do and need to serve the ladies over cards. You will hear all the gossip and see all the fine clothes, and I shall have nothing to do but listen to Lady Mary tell us about her last lying-in!'

Dorcas smirked. 'Lady Hester knows who to trust and I know what the gentlemen have.' She softened. 'We have time for our supper before they serve the soup, and there's a nice bit of pasty left from Sir Edwin's dinner that wants eating.'

'I'll set it out, Dorcas. You have enough to do, with Abbie as she is, but I have to go back for five minutes to see that Lady Hester has everything she needs.'

Once more, Hope climbed the back stairs and hurried to the boudoir. Hester looked up from the escritoire where she was writing a note and waved Hope away with a vague gesture when she suggested that she might help Abigail and have her supper in the kitchen. 'Come back only to undress me when I retire,' she said, and Hope walked along the corridor towards the back stairs, suddenly very hungry.

Voices from the Great Hall made her hesitate. She crept back to the dark gallery above the hall and looked down at the three blazing fires and the glint of arms on the walls, reflected in the brightness. A manservant was lighting more candles, and by one of the fires, a pair of long legs stretched out to the warmth. The mudstained breeches and damp tunic were rich and colourful, the small beard was trim under full, firm lips and the eyes that now looked up into the darkness of the gallery were filled with curiosity, even though the face was tired from the chase.

Hope drew back into darker shadow, her heart beating rapidly as she feared discovery since Lady Hester had forbidden her to be seen by the men, but she was fascinated by the man in the hall below. More candles were lit and a glint of auburn was released from the curling hair. The velvet cap, tossed idly onto a settle, glowed with the lustre of the huge gold pin in the shape of a crossbow that sat by its fellow, another pin in the shape of a beautifully wrought handgun. Hope crept away, carrying the picture in her mind of the foreign clothes and elegant figure of the young man who had hunted with Sir Edwin that day and had brought news of Charles, the son of the Clinton household, now in France on the Grand Tour.

Jerard Barill stared into the darkness above the gallery, then smiled. The day had been good with rare sport and good company, the evening promised good food and wine and now he was seeing visions. Or at least a fleeting vision of dark eyes in a pale, heart-shaped face that seemed to float over the air like a wraith. The daughter of the house? A visitor? He dragged his weary limbs out of the slung leather seat and went to the room he shared with two other huntsmen. At supper, it would be interesting to make her acquaintance. If her figure matched her face, she was a beauty to match any he had met in the valley of the Rhône and on his travels.

# II

John Levett slid from the mare and led her to the trough by the pump and watched her drink. Three women at the conduit by the way to Vicar's Close dragged heavy buckets that slopped water over the cobbles as they walked slowly home and were met by two other women with yokes and empty buckets.

'Finished at the palace, John?'

'The mews are nearly empty, and most of the horses are hidden in farm stalls and bothies until we see which way the wind blows here. I had but four to shoe and a bit of harness to mend and the Canon said he would be in Burton for the next four months.'

'He would,' sniffed Jane Willow. 'A fat belly, but no stomach for trouble.'

'There's news of men and musketry beyond Warwick under Lord Grenville Brooke,' John reported. 'By all accounts he gathers more and more from the south and is set to come this way.' He tugged at the reins to make the mare pause for breath as she was hot and might be bloated if she drank too much cold water.

'The south!' derided Jane, as if all pestilence and trouble came from the South. 'Last night more wagons with arms came through Lichfield from the northern ports for the King, but they say it will be a miracle if they reach Oxford where the court lies.'

'Better get your herbs ready, Jane. We might need soothing balms if the Roundheads carry mortars,' he laughed. 'I think we grow too cautious. If we go about our given work, we can fear no man or creed.'

'If they are Roundheads wounded, they'll get more than sweet herbs from me,' she said, tartly. 'Will you fight, John? You show no favour for Cromwell and yet never speak for the King.'

'I would fight to defend my own and my friends,' he said simply. 'Men with pikes and guns are all alike in my reckoning and the first who tries to take my cottage or my nags can expect a hammering. Good day, Lucy,' he said and his face deepened in colour as Jane's daughter dragged her buckets clear of the conduit and hitched them to her yoke.

'What if the Roundheads come and demand your service as a farrier, John?' Her expression was anxious but she showed none of the awareness that John obviously felt for her.

'If they give me money bearing the King's head, I'll shoe their horses,' he said with a grin, 'and if the Royalists come, then I'll make their hooves as good as new with an extra polish to them. Parliament rules us in London but they won't think we are important enough to come here.' He eased the girth and led the mare away from the trough.

'I was in the cathedral this morning, cleaning the brass, and heard many rumours,' Lucy said with a scared glance at her mother. 'The canons have prepared a place of refuge within the walls and made sure that the portcullis and heavy doors swing true. The say that Cromwell's men have been seen in Warwick and that some are here in disguise to find the lie of the land.'

'There's one who is here now,' said Jane, and nudged her daughter to make her keep quiet. 'Well, Francis; it's a long time since you troubled our city.' She eyed the tall, thin man who had appeared as if from nowhere and who stood listening to all they said.

Francis Turner scowled. 'I came to see my parents as any son must,' he said.

'And to spy on the cathedral?'

'If my mother slaves for the church and my father has a care of the moat and grounds, why shouldn't I come here to find them?' he asked sarcastically.

John regarded him in silence, taking in the dark sober tunic and breeches and the wide hat that had become the uniform of the Puritans. He saw too a deep crease and the stain of leather left from a discarded bandolier and the rub of a sword hilt at the man's side. Francis Turner a soldier? But not broadcasting the fact in his own city?

'Your mother has missed you, Francis,' said Lucy in an attempt to make him smile. 'It must set her mind at rest to see you in these troubled times.'

'They'll be safe enough when the Protector comes,' he boasted. He glanced at Jane balefully. 'There are some who should mind their steps. Parliament has no time for witches.'

'Jane is no witch,' said John. 'When has she ever done harm to anyone?'

'Witches and fornicators and adulterers will be brought to justice when Lord Cromwell has the whole country in his hand.' Francis spoke as if he would personally enjoy enforcing such laws and Lucy turned pale. 'I had a horse that sickened after I left it in Quonians Lane,' he went on. 'It grazed in the field at the back of your cottage and nearly died.'

'I thought we'd settled that score with our fists,' said John. 'You bought it cheap and bought trouble with it. You never could judge horse flesh Francis, and ever since we were infants you've thought you were God Almighty, especially when you were in the wrong! That field stretches past your cottage too, and behind your plot there's sour grass and poisonous plants enough to kill a herd of cattle.'

Francis Turner rubbed his jaw as though the pain lingered from the blows that he had suffered from John's fists. 'Don't worry. You'll be safe enough, and all the Levetts, John,' he sneered. 'Sam is a good man and true to the cause and Hope will make a fine wife for an honest man.'

'Hope is safe,' said John with satisfaction. 'And I can fight my own battles if need be. I owe nothing to any cause and am a good farrier and that is enough. Men will want their horses shod long after they have shot down a few enemies in anger.'

'Hope is not here?' Francis lost his superior air.

'You've been away a year,' said John. 'Hope is out along the way to Alrewas and has been these four months.'

'The Clintons?' Francis turned away to hide his anger. 'Sam promised me I'd have her when I came back and I thought to wed this Easter time.'

'*Sam* said? What of the girl?' Jane laughed. 'She wouldn't want you, Francis Turner. She's got more sense than to tie

24

herself to a man like her own father.' She nodded sagely. 'I hear things in Quonians Lane and she's well out of it. Lucy misses her, but I'm glad she's found a good place with honest people.'

'I do miss her,' Lucy agreed. 'If the weather was warmer I'd walk over to see her. She was here for a day or so but went back before we had time together as the cathedral needed Mother and me to settle the silver and the vestment boxes after Christmas. The Bishop's robes had to be sewn up in fresh linen to keep out the dust, and the aisles were heavy with mud.'

'I'll take you, Lucy. There's little to do now they've moved the horses and I can take you pillion for half a day.' John looked more animated, and Lucy smiled at him.

'Bring some victuals so we don't put a drain on Hope if they dislike feeding strangers, and I can take some more of her clothes that she left behind.'

'I pass that way,' said Francis. 'I can take what she needs.'

'As her brother, I think Lady Hester will welcome me more than just any man who lusts after her maid,' said John grimly. He gave a short laugh. 'Going north, Francis? No wonder you take care to hide your arms and ammunition. That garb might shut a few mouths in the inns if you ask too many questions. The Earl of Newcastle guards convoys and the tongues of his men when such as you appear.'

Francis walked away and they watched him climb on to the saddle of a fine bay mare. The harness was of the best and the panniers heavy and covered with well-tooled leather. John grinned. The Parliamentarians shouted the virtues of poverty and equality but took what they wanted for themselves. He wondered which rich estate had been rifled to give Francis such booty.

The thought sobered him. Lady Hester Clinton made no secret of her wealth and dressed in fine clothes when she came to Lichfield in the huge yellow carriage with dark green velvet cushions, the same colour as the livery of the coachman and footmen. Perhaps he was too confident that Hope would be safe in the care of the Clintons. Her whole appearance had changed with the gift of the good gown and shoes and the means to keep her hands soft with less heavy work. Inwardly he wished that his sister was plain and fat and inconspicuous, and resolved to lecture her when he saw her again. The belief that the Royalists would come to guard Lichfield was fading, and a girl in dark worsted and demure linen fichu might be less provocative to the coarse soldiers with Cromwell.

'How did honest folk like Daniel and Meg Turner spawn a child like Francis?' asked Jane. 'I work with Meg in the church and she never says a bad thing about anyone and yet suffers enough with her joints to try a saint. I made a salve of angelica and bay in good white wax that gives her some ease, and she takes a draught of willow bark and gout weed when the pain is bad, but that makes her ears buzz so she takes it only in small doses.'

'You'd better be careful that she doesn't have anything to upset her while Francis is here,' said Lucy. 'He has an evil mind and could bring us harm.'

'He's only an ignorant soldier. Must be to come here and think we don't know what he's been doing this last year. My herbs never hurt anyone and as for spells and witchcraft, I wouldn't want to sup with the Devil.'

John glanced up at the sky and then at Lucy. She smiled. 'We could go today, Mother. The weather seems set.' She turned to

John. 'If you carry my buckets I'll get some bread and cheese to take and be ready in half an hour.'

John slung the yoke over his shoulders as if he were carrying feathers and the mare followed him as he walked to Quonians Lane, to the timber and plaster cottage where Lucy lived with her mother. In his own home, John was relieved to find his father not there, but suspected that he was with Francis Turner, three cottages along the row where the bay mare was tethered to a post. Birds of a feather, he thought, and made a neat bundle of all Hope's other worldy goods. He put a flagon of ale in one saddlebag and was ready to lift his pillion passenger up behind him when Lucy came with a small basket of food and a thick cloak against the cold.

The fowling piece he slung across the saddle was old but well oiled and tended, and a coil of rope weighted with heavy lead at each end hung from the pommel, a weapon he had learned to use when a relative of the Duke of Buckingham returned from overseas and showed him at Bartholomew's fair how the cattle men brought down calves and steers by means of the bolas.

The mud had set firm after three clear days with no rain and the air smelled of winter's leaves and cattle dung as they passed farmyards and reached the road through woodland. The bare branches gave no cover to footpads, but John kept a watchful eye on the thickets and Lucy clung to his waist in an effort to keep warm. 'Hold on tight,' he said. 'I'll look after you, Lucy.' His voice was soft and the tone like the one he used when gentling an unbroken colt.

'I know, John,' she whispered. 'You are a good man.' The broad back was comforting and for the first time, Lucy felt a warmth that she had never experienced. Their bodies were close and the horse's pace made her press even closer, her breasts tight against John's back. She felt shy and was glad he couldn't see her face. The mild amusement she had felt over the past year, knowing his dumb devotion, left her and she wondered what it would be like if she married him.

A ruined chapel, which had once been a part of a great church estate before the monastery had been razed at the dissolution, gave them shelter while they ate the bread and cheese, washed down with John's own ale. Lucy stretched to ease her stiff legs then fetched the basket to set out the food on a long flat stone while John found straw stacked in a shed and brought it to make a dry seat.

'I haven't been in here since I was a lad,' he said, grinning. 'We used to come with firebrands and smoke out the bats in that old tower.' He kicked at some blackened stones. 'We aren't the only ones to shelter here. That fire must have been lit over the past week or so. Look how light the ash is and how it stays piled even with the draught.' He frowned.

'What's wrong, John?'

'Nowt that I can say, but there've been men with armour here.' He handed over a piece of steel. 'I've riveted a few of those. It's from a facepiece of a helmet, and if I'm true to what I know, I'd say it was Roundhead armour.' He walked further into the ruins to a snug place protected by a wall and well roofed. 'Three men have slept here, look at that!' Three well-defined depressions in a heap of straw made Lucy stare into the dark corners as if the men might still be there.

'Do you think they'll come back?' she asked with a quaver in her voice.

28

'No. They've been here briefly and passed on,' said John. 'They left nothing and made little disturbance and didn't want to be seen here.' He smirked. 'A good hiding-place, as few pass close enough to look inside, but they missed a better one. If I remember aright, there's a big cellar, a kind of crypt like under the cathedral, and it comes out at the back.'

He made for the crumbling stone heaped beyond the old vestry but Lucy clutched his sleeve. 'No, John! They may have found it and be there.'

He turned and saw the tears in her eyes and his face glowed with sudden delight. 'You'd care if I was killed, my girl?' She nodded and raised her face for their first kiss. 'I'll look after you,' he whispered after a long five minutes. 'I swear that you and your mother will be safe from whoever comes to Lichfield, under whatever banner.' He thought of Jane and her sudden acid tongue, and her herbs. 'There might be a time when Jane is harassed,' he said. 'Remember this, Lucy.' He pushed aside an old beam of heavy oak that lay across a broken doorway. Under it lay a pile of dust and loose stones. John grunted with satisfaction. 'It hasn't been disturbed for years.' Effortlessly, he raised a slab and Lucy saw steps leading down and round to an underground chamber.

The air was quite fresh and at the end of the big room another short flight of steps led them to a wooden door set in a wall. With difficulty, John shifted the latch and it opened inwards, leaving the dense bed of nettles that hid it from outside view undisturbed. He closed the door and leaned loose boards against it, hiding it from casual inspection, then took Lucy back to the vestry. 'See if you can move the stone,' he said.

'It slides as if oiled,' said Lucy with surprise. She slid it back again with ease and then put it firmly over the hole.

'Remember this place in case you or Jane have need of it.' John kicked loose rubble over the slab and added a few lengths of timber for good measure. 'There. Tell no one of this place, not even your mother or my own sister,' he said sternly, and held her close as if to keep her from any breath of trouble. 'I shall bring a keg of water and some ale one day soon and hide it down there.'

'You really believe we might have to come here?'

'You will feel safer knowing that there is a refuge,' he replied simply. 'Nobody knows about this place but us.'

'What of the friends who came here with you to smoke out the bats?' she asked.

'Only a few of us found that place and they will have forgotten long since,' he replied, and tried to ignore the inner voice that told him the name of one who had played there and fought there and who might have a good memory.

The road opened out beyond the wood and the manor house came into view against a bright cold sky, no longer hidden by the leaves of the trees that in summer made a screen and concealed the rambling buildings. John pressed his heels into the flanks of the mare and she went more quickly along the gravelled way to the stables. A boy came out and took the bridle, grinning when he saw who rode the mare. 'We're hard put for stalls, Master Levett, but I'll find you a snug corner and a bite of fodder in the barn.'

He directed them to the kitchen and took the horse as soon as John emptied the saddlebags. From an upper window Sir Edwin saw them and sent word that he would see John Levett in the Great Hall, and to tell Hope that her brother was there and that she might come down after Sir Edwin had finished talking to him.

Lucy sat by the kitchen fire and waited while John was away. Abigail gave her buttermilk and a slice of spiced bun and asked for news about Lichfield. 'I hear the Roundheads are ducking any woman who won't lie with them and hanging those who do,' said Abbie, as if it were all a huge joke. 'So you'd best look out if they come your way.'

'Cromwell hasn't reached Lichfield, Abbie,' said Lucy, the warmth and tasty bun making her feel secure. 'Men like John will see that they don't get a foothold and the King has forces enough that can come from Oxford if we need them.'

'The groom heard yesterday that Lord Cromwell is gathering men and arms fast at Warwick,' said Abbie, who showed no sign of her last night's drinking and was now eager for gossip. 'There's nothing they say when out hunting that Silas misses, and the gentry must think that all grooms are deaf, the things they say when he is there and taking it all in. If he was a spy they'd be in The Tower half the time,' she added. 'Sir Edwin doesn't agree with everything the King does, even if he is loyal and would give his life in battle for the Crown.'

'And does he tell you?' enquired Lucy, intrigued by the goings-on in the great house.

'My good ale unloosens many tongues,' said Abbie. 'Mine too, may the Lord forgive me. I say things and can't remember the half of it when I'm sober, so don't tell me any secrets!'

'I won't,' said Lucy. looking eagerly to the door when she heard it open. I may not tell *you*, she thought, but I must tell Hope about John and me, and when Hope ran into the kitchen, they hugged as if they had not seen each other for months.

'What brings you here?' asked Hope. 'Nothing bad? Is Jane in good health?'

'All is well, the pump hasn't dried and the cathedral hasn't burned down.' Lucy laughed and Abbie ambled away to fetch barley wine and bread. Lucy glanced at her retreating back and whispered, 'John and me want to be married.'

'Then we'll be real sisters,' said Hope, her eyes sparkling with pleasure. 'I thought him slow in asking, but I'm glad.'

'I wish you'd marry, too, and come back to Lichfield,' said Lucy wistfully. 'I miss you there, and life seems dull now with everyone looking back over their shoulders as if Cromwell will pounce on them or the Royalists will take their horses. When it comes to it, there's naught to choose between two bands of fighting men,' she added with a burst of wisdom.

Hope shrugged. 'Who would I marry, Lucy? Not Francis Turner, that's for certain, even if . . . my father . . . beats me for refusing. I'm happy here, and Lady Hester is good to me. I want nothing better than to live here in peace and serve her.' She moved restlessly and her eyes were dreamy. 'There's no one I could marry.'

'Take care, Hope. It's safer to be married. In a house like this, gentlemen take maids like us for their pleasure and leave a lot of grief behind them.'

'I am to be more than a servant, Lucy. Lady Hester has made me her companion, and next week, after the visitors leave, I shall have everything befitting that position. Tell nobody but John, and keep it from Sam Levett.' Hope found it no longer possible to refer to Sam as her father and each time she thought of him, she rejoiced to think she was not of his blood.

Abbie called that she was wanted in the Great Hall and Hope left the kitchen to find her brother. John turned from the fire as soon as he heard her come in and took her into a bear hug. 'You look well,' he said. 'Quite the lady, too.' He eyed the gown that Hope had just finished making from dark red wool that Lady Hester had found too deep for her delicate complexion and had set the linen keeper and Hope to cut out and sew. It added to the other garments that had begun to make a handsome collection for the girl.

They talked of his betrothal and of Hope's new standing in the household. 'I shall see you when Lady Hester wants to go to Lichfield, but I'm glad you brought the rest of my things because I shall never step into that cottage again if Sam is there,' Hope vowed. 'Don't look like that, John. I know that I am not his daughter and it gives me relief. I'd rather be the bastard of a gentleman than of his bedding.'

'I'd like to see you safely wed,' John told her. He looked about him at the good furniture and heavy wall hangings and the bright silver and brass on the table and chest. 'This is not yours,' he said bluntly. 'It's easy to think so but whatever your birth, you don't have any claim to fortune. Be careful with love, and listen to no fine words and flattery. It's just one path to the one our mother took and brought nothing but misery to her.' He grinned. 'You may be in the fire here, but you've escaped worse. Francis Turner was in the city asking for you and seemed to think you are promised to him.'

Hope tossed her head and looked angry. 'He knows I would never marry him,' she said. 'He's a ne'er-do-well and a liar.'

'Be careful,' said John, more seriously. 'He's well in with the Parliament troops and I think has joined the ranks. He rides a

fine horse with good trappings and swaggers as he did when
he had the biggest apple! I doubt if he'll come here but happen
he will if Oliver's men come this way. He's the crow that
hangs back until it thinks there's defenceless carrion to peck
and then takes over. He talks of Cromwell as the Protector and
bragged that his own name should be Leveller.'

'Why's that?'

'They are a radical set within the Puritans who think that all
men are equal, and want to kill all who have rank through
birth, and to raze all churches. They grow so fanatical that
even Parliament is slow to own their allegiance as they could
grow to be a thorn in the side instead of an aid to victory.'

'Have you had dinner?' asked Hope.

'We brought our own,' said John. 'We ate it in the old chapel
a couple of miles along the road.'

'I remember! We played there as children and you slapped
me when I wanted to climb the old tower.'

'It's still dangerous. Men have been using it as shelter and I
found this.'

'What have you there?'

John turned to see who had spoken to him and saw that Sir
Edwin had re-entered the room.

'A rivet and broken piece from a visor, Sir Edwin. None of
yours, I don't think. I found it in the woods on the way from
Lichfield where men had slept in the ruins. Three men by the
signs, sir, and they were careful to leave no fire or ordure, like
men in secret, on the move.'

'I'll have a watch set along the road tonight,' said Sir Edwin.
He turned the metal in his hand. 'They come close,' he said in
a low voice. 'I should drill my men and stop all hunting for

pleasure.' He gave John a keen look. 'You work with metal: how are you with guns? I came down again to ask you to look at a stallion and to see his hooves. He's young and not yet shod, and my men are frightened to hold him for shoeing. I've ordered a furnace to be hot and we have anvils and hammers enough. Will you see to him today? Then while you wait for the right heat, look at my armoury and advise my steward.'

'Can he be tired before I go to him? The groom must walk him and trot him round on a rein for an hour and then have a warm mash ready to make him content while I handle him.' Sir Edwin nodded and called for his steward to give the order. 'Your sister may take you for food and drink, then come to the armoury. I must see to my guests. We have a fine shot with us and he brought down more game than we can use. Can you take a deer to the cathedral and some for your own use?'

'I brought Lucy Willow as pillion to see Hope,' said John. 'I can ride here tomorrow and bring a nag on a bridle to carry whatever you want me to take.'

'No, you can have one of my mules and keep it until you come again. A brace of good fat deer will hang well in the close and be food in an emergency. When you come again, bring me the things I have listed from the arsenal. I've put my seal to it and you will be served well, but first tell me what more we need for defence.' He strode away and Hope heard voices and the whinny of a horse impatient to be off. She heard the horse-men ride away and wondered if the foreign gentleman had gone for good. Sir Edwin returned to the house, and John ate his fill of liver and bread before looking over the guns.

# III

'My husband talks of going to London,' said Lady Hester. Her cousin, Sir Tristram Hinter, nodded. 'He has told you?' She paced the room and looked worried.

'Have no fear, Hester. Oliver hasn't lost all his senses. He needs money as much as the King and he knows that even if he seized land and good houses, the wealth of men like Edwin isn't as easy to take. The estates in Scotland and Ireland and the vineyards in France and Germany are enough to make a tethered dog's mouth water when they are out of reach and force will do nothing to bring them closer. Edwin hasn't fought in this trouble, and is known only to defend his own and not to pick a quarrel, so he's safe enough if he takes arms and men with him, just as he would against highwaymen and cutpurses even in peacetime.'

'You think the King will be defeated and have to accept the changes made by Parliament?'

'He has already made concessions and summoned Parliament after the long break even if it ended with neither side satisfied. We have a king and nothing can deny his Divine Right, and when the dust settles, they'll need men like Edwin to help the economy. You can't break everything if there's nothing to put in its place,' he said bluntly. 'Whatever the Protector says, he will need us, and he'll have to tone down all the rantings of his fanatics.' He sighed. 'There'll be milk spilled before that. They dragged a girl through Warwick in a white sheet and ducked her for fornicating. They say it was one of their soldiers who raped her, but he was let off and blamed the girl for tempting him. The power of petty men is more dangerous than an army of honest soldiers, and the witch hunt condemns many who are but the target of jealousy and personal spite.'

Sir Tristram tried to console her when he saw her anguish, but she waved away his change of tone. 'I must know the truth, Cousin. I have the care of many servants and fear for those who open their mouths too wide in the ale houses. Already there have been fights and many who envy the rich think that Cromwell will give them riches, they grow bold and poach and pilfer, saying that all men are equal, until they are caught and then they know it is not so.'

'I stayed to be with Edwin today. The others have gone over to Fradley Wood to flush out hares but I think that Edwin needs me to go with him. A bigger band of men will make the journey safe and carry more authority, and we have the hand of Parliament on our document of safe passage.' He shrugged. 'It may have been signed when Edwin believed that new laws would bring light and peace to the country, before he knew of the excesses of the Roundheads, but it will keep us in good stead on this journey, and if we can gain protection for Lichfield we shall not have sold ourselves to an anti-Christ.'

'Even Cromwell would never attack the cathedral,' Hester

almost laughed. 'That would be a sin against God and the Crown and against the wishes of the people. What would he gain by it? There are houses with arms that must attract him more, and farms with full barns to feed hungry soldiers.'

'The canons have full barns, madam; and fish ponds and cattle and hens aplenty. Men on the rampage know no difference between a hen laying eggs in the Cathedral Close and one bred by a pagan. Lock your doors and make fast the shutters when we are away, madam. These are uneasy times.'

Hester walked along the gallery with him. 'Where is my husband?' she asked.

'Below with a farrier from Lichfield who is to shoe the new stallion. It was fortuitous. He came with a wench to visit one of your servants and has been put to good use.'

'John Levett here?' Hester smiled. 'He must have brought a neighbour to see his sister, my maid.' She looked down into the Great Hall and saw Hope talk to her brother, then gather up the bundles he had brought. The girl went by the back stairs to her room and Lady Hester went down to speak to John.

'My lady!' he said, and grinned. 'I brought the rest of Hope's bits and pieces, and Lucy Willow to see her.'

'And my husband put you to work.' Hester shook her head. 'You are too good at your work, John. We could use you here all the time.'

'It might come to that,' muttered John.

'What did you say?'

'There's little work in the close now, Lady Hester. The canons have sent away as many of the horses as can be spared and so I have time to visit like a squire. I've farmed out two of

39

my nags as it doesn't matter who comes, they will take our horses. In Birmingham, they walk,' he added grimly. 'And if they had mounts they would have to put them to grass, as oats and barley have been taken for the troops and with men away fighting, the seed corn lies sprouting in the bins.' He sighed. 'We've had bad harvests these last three years after such plenty we didn't know what to do with it, and now we shall starve if the men don't go back to the plough.'

'We have stores,' said Hester, 'and even if soldiers come along the road from Warwick, they will not come here, unless they are Prince Rupert's men from the north, and he is a gentleman, who would not allow thieving and coarse behaviour.'

'There be as many bastards left behind after troops pass by whatever army they come from,' said John. 'As many broken heads and empty larders, and the leaders turn a blind eye. I'm glad that Hope is here, my lady. I know she is safe with you and I wish my Lucy was as safe.'

'Your Lucy?' Hester raised an amused eyebrow. 'You have at last asked for her?' She saw his shocked expression. 'We may be miles from Lichfield but I hear the gossip. In fact, that's why I came down to see you, to hear what is being said at the pump by Dean's Walk. More truth comes from my servants than ever comes from the church dignitaries who come to sup with us here.'

'There are some who preach against the church and for Cromwell, my lady. Francis Turner is one, and I think he has taken arms even when he says he comes but to visit as the son of Meg and Daniel Turner, and I have fears for Jane Willow, the mother of my Lucy, who deals in herbs and potions and has the cut of a wise woman, but with a tongue that rubs like sand. Francis hates her and would do her harm. I have fought with him in the past and my fists itch each time I see him.'

Hope stopped in the doorway when she caught sight of Lady Hester, who turned when she saw John smile. 'You may see your brother later. My husband needs him in the stables now and asked for a warm bran mash. Take it to them if you don't mind the smell of burning hoof, and come to me later when you are free of the stable smell.'

Hope fetched an old cloak from the bundle that John had brought, wondering how she had ever been satisfied with the shabby clothes she once wore, but it hid her good gown, and the shoes she now wore had seen mud enough in the past not to matter in the mire of the stable yard. The heavy bucket of mash smelled fragrant and as she passed the stalls of the other other horses, they sniffed the air and whinnied.

John and the Master were leaning over the half-door of a big stall where a handsome stallion nosed some hay. His flanks heaved slightly after the vigorous exercise to tire him, but he looked as if he had energy and more to spare. The groom passed a halter round the beast's neck and tethered him firmly, hobbling the front legs, while another lad gentled him. John ran a firm hand down the horse's haunches and spoke in a low voice, tracing the hard excess horn and measuring for a shoe. He stripped off his shirt and the sound of hammer on hot metal rang through the stables as he shaped and flattened the red-hot shoe.

The groom showed the mash to the horse and held it just away from his muzzle, so that he concentrated on that and not on what was happening behind him. John trimmed the horn with a sharp knife and filed the hoof, holding it in a grip that seemed to reassure the beast. A sharp sizzling sound and the smell of burning and the first shoe was in place, quickly secured by the long nails that John now held in his mouth ready to take one at a time and hammer home, as the mash was held close enough to the greedy mouth to be taken.

As always, Hope was fascinated by the process and watched each shoe as it came from the forge never seeming to worry the horse with its heat. Her face glowed with pleasure and from the heat of the small forge behind her, then she felt that someone was looking at her and turned slightly. In the doorway was the man she had seen at ease in the Hall. He seemed puzzled as if he knew her but could not put a name to her. His attention, however, was mostly on the horse and he watched the farrier's easy strength with admiration.

To reach the stable yard, Hope had to pass the man who now wore his velvet hat at a rakish angle and resembled a prince. She wondered what Lord Cromwell would make of the elegant and richly attired young man, and what any of the ladies of the Court would make of his arrogance and good looks. A wistful feeling made her sad. In these clothes, she thought, he merely glances at me but then watches a horse! He could have any woman he wanted, she thought. Even Abbie knew that, and would gladly have given him anything he wanted, if his pride took him so low.

The last nail went in the last shoe and the man at the door took off his hat and waved it in salute. *'Magnifique, mon brave,'* he said.

John couldn't understand his words but there was no doubt about the meaning. He wiped the sweat from his eyes. Sir

Edwin held out a pot of ale and clapped him on the back. 'As gentle as a lamb today in your hands, Levett. I am well satisfied. I thought to have had a broken limb or two here while they held him.'

'Keep away from his hooves,' John suggested. 'First irons are heavy and he may try to shed them. A bale or two of straw by the wood may save the doors and a good gallop later will calm him for the night.' He saw Hope waiting to speak to him and so dragged on his shirt. Jerard Barill strolled over to join them and eyed Hope with ill-concealed admiration and curiosity. Her shabby cloak hung back revealing the red gown with the delicate lace at the bosom.

'Last night you were . . . *malade*, Mademoiselle? Ill?'

'No, sir,' Hope said.

'You did not sup with Lady Hester and us. I saw your face in the gallery. Are you the daughter of the house?'

'She is my sister,' said John, his smile fading. 'She is under the protection of Lady Hester and in my care, too.'

'I am to be Lady Hester's companion,' said Hope with pride, forgetting that her mistress had ordered her to say nothing about her new position for a while.

'Companion? *Un chaperon*?' He laughed. 'It is Lady Hester, *non*, who is *le chaperon* for one so *fraîche, si ravissant*?'

'This is Hope Levett, my boy,' said Sir Edwin. 'She is my wife's companion and lady's maid.' He gave the young man a serious glance. 'She is not a domestic to be taken lightly. She is of good family.' He spoke rapidly in French and Jerard's expression lost its flirtatious edge.

John put on his coat and looked up at the sky. 'It's late Sir Edwin, and we must get back. It will be dark and cold before we reach Lichfield, and Lucy gets frightened of the shapes along the road.'

'It's too late to start out now, Levett. Stay and help me get my horses ready for my journey to London. I leave at first light and you can have some time with your sister.'

John eyed the handsome foreigner and then nodded. Hope was twisting the edge of her cloak between her fingers as she had done ever since she was a small child when anything worried her, and the bold look in the gentleman's dark eyes, openly admiring her, made John uneasy. 'We'll stay,' he said. 'Go and tell Lucy, and if Lady Hester doesn't mind, she can sleep in your room.'

Hope tried to pass the men without touching Jerard Barill, but as she went by, he seized her hand and kissed it. Scarlet-faced, she fled to the safety of the house, pulled off her cloak and shoes and sat on her hard bed, her breath coming unevenly and her pulse racing. She went down the back stairs to find Lucy who was nervously watching the dark clouds scudding across the evening sky, making the darkness deep and forbidding. Together, they helped prepare supper for the family and then sat with Abbie and the maids to eat theirs. John came in with the head groom and coachman and ate with them with much laughter, and with Abbie not so drunk as to be bad-tempered, but drunk enough to tell bawdy tales and to make them laugh.

From time to time, Hope thought of the man whose touch had made her tremble. The soft brush of careless lips over her hand and the scent of his clothes remained with her. Tomorrow, he would be gone with Sir Edwin and she would forget him. Tomorrow, something would leave her life with an empty space that could not be filled by work or clothes or the company of her friends.

Lucy slept well on the small truckle bed and woke only when Hope shook her and told her that there was ale and bread in the kitchen and that John might want to get back to Lichfield early. Lady Hester was awake and in her robe to say goodbye to her husband, with many tears and admonitions to be careful, to keep well and to remember to drink sack against chills and the plague. She gave him powder to put in beds where there could be fleas in any dirty inns he might have to use, and looked apprehensive when he belted on his hand-guns and bullets and sheathed his sword, although she had seen him do so a hundred times before.

At last he left the boudoir and Hester tidied up her jewel case. Hope went down to have the first draught of the day and a piece of bread, and heard the men leaving. John came to the kitchen smiling, and ate heartily, well pleased with the money given him for his services and by the praise of the other men in the party. 'The Frenchie sits a horse well,' he said. 'As fine a beast as I saw anywhere and such trappings! Just as well the Puritans can't see him. He's like a bird of paradise.'

'Has he gone back to France?' asked Lucy.

'Not yet. He hopes to see the King in Oxford but can go to London too, as a diplomat, or so Sir Edwin said,' the coach-man told them. 'I hope he can defend himself if he runs into trouble. A bit of paper won't stop a bullet!'

'He's handy with horses,' said John, 'and wears badges to show he can fight with guns and a crossbow. Sir Edwin asked him to tell us how he came by the gold pins in his hat, and it seems they have contests where he lives and they make the best of them the King of the Crossbow, and King of the Small Arms. He has both so he must be good.'

Hope drank in every mention of Jerard Barill. Was he a nobleman? What rank did the French give to their sons? He was of a wealthy family, that was clear from his dress and manners, but he could make men like John, who had no time for frills, talk to him and share as equals, work and pleasure, and it was plain to see that in spite of his first distrust, John had been easy with him. She started at what was John saying: *When* he comes back?

'The Frenchman. You think he will come back here?' she asked carelessly.

'You were in a cloud, my girl. I was saying he is coming back and then I'll show him how to throw a calf with my rope. He's seen it done in Spain but never had time to try it.'

'I have to go to my lady,' said Hope, and embraced Lucy. 'Make John bring you again, and stay if Lady Hester says you may.' She kissed her and urged her to be married soon. 'It isn't safe for you and Jane to live alone in that cottage,' Hope said. 'With John to protect you, I shall be easy and he can leave Sam Levett and have a real home and some comfort.'

She watched Lucy smile up into John's face and envied her. A simple girl, newly in love with a good simple man, and they would marry and have many children. She thought of the lads in Quonians Lane and in the cottages by the Close. None of them meant anything to her apart from being her friends, and the sons of the gentry eyed her with lust but none of them would consider marrying her.

She walked erect. I am no servant. I am the companion of Lady Hester Clinton and as such will have more respect. But

46

her shoulders sagged as she recalled the wickedly exciting man who had kissed her hand and she no longer condemned her mother for weakness of the flesh. My grandmother was taken by force, but I must have been born of love, she thought dreamily. It was a relief that Sam Levett was not her father and she rubbed soothing salve into her hands before going to Lady Hester.

'They are gone,' said Lady Hester with an air of tragedy. 'When shall I see my husband again alive?'

'Let me brush your hair, madam,' suggested Hope, and drew the silver-backed brushes through the abundant fair tresses in a smooth rhythm that soothed both of them. I can't show my concern except for my master and the other men with him. I have no right to weep for the safety of a man I do not know.

Hester sighed. 'That calms me as nothing else can do, but there is work to be done. Edwin left a list of orders to be given to the groom and the farm hands, and the rooms that the gentlemen used must be put to rights. Make sure that the maid sweeps the floors and brings out any tankards and dishes that may have been left there. They used three rooms on the other side of the gallery, and we may have use for them again soon.'

The maid took up her besom and swept the first of the rooms. 'I'll gather the dirty dishes and take them down to the kitchen,' said Hope. 'Then you must wash away this patch of spilled wine.' She heaped the soiled linen into a wicker basket and took the first tray of dishes down to Abbie and the kitchen maids, then went back for more.

The second room was in better order than the first, as if the person who had slept there was more fastidious. At least one corner was neat and had no wine stains on the polished floor, and the bed linen smelled not of a man's sweat but of something that Hope remembered from the perfume on the clothes worn by the Frenchman. She pulled the linen from the bed and held it as if it were a living thing, her eyes half shut, then caught a glimpse of something bright that had been hidden by the overhanging spread. She reached down and picked up a gold pin in the shape of a crossbow and turned it over in her fingers. On the back was an inscription in French which she could not understand but she could read the name *Jerard Barill*.

The clasp was loose and had slipped back, and Hope put the brooch in her pocket to give to Lady Hester for safekeeping. The maid called her to help make up the beds with fresh linen, and Hope had no time to wonder about the pin and why the name was simply Jerard Barill, with no title and no hint of rank.

# IV

Men stared at the sight of the mule, laden with the three carcasses of deer, and the bulging saddlebags of the leading, horse. John laughed. 'They think we've spent the night poaching,' he said. 'But it would take a brave man to flaunt his kill through Dam Street in broad daylight.' He rode along Quonians Lane and left one of the deer in the cottage with Jane and Lucy before taking the others to Cathedral Close. 'I'll not leave good venison with my father,' he said. 'He'd take it and sell it, and I have better uses for it among my friends and the needy.'

The sight of the good meat did much to make Jane better tempered. Her fears for them had grown through the night when they didn't return from the manor, and rumours were spreading that Lord Grenville Brooke, one of Cromwell's most fanatical followers, had been seen along the Birmingham Road with a band of soldiers and that they were marching towards Lichfield.

'You stay in, my maid,' she told Lucy. 'Let John find out what is afoot and come back quickly and tell us.' She stirred a pot that emitted a very unpleasant smell, and John sniffed and turned up his nose. 'It's not your dinner,' she said. 'I'm brewing a poultice for someone and she'll be here any minute, so get you gone and bring us back some firm news.' She turned back to the pot, glancing sharply at Lucy. 'Now tell me the news of the manor and what you've been up to with that John Levett.'

John Levett looked up to the three graceful spires of the cathedral that had been the centre of his life since he was a child. Most of the townsfolk depended on the rich community for livelihood and tended the moat, the fabric of the huge building and the cluster of houses where the dignitaries of the church lived in peace and luxury. The two great ponds provided fish, and the bakers, tanners and victuallers in business near the great church made Lichfield a busy and prosperous city that any country could envy. He was happy. Lucy loved him and they would wed before June; Hope was going to be a fine lady if she stayed with the Clintons and behaved herself; and he stood high in the regard of men like Sir Edwin, his coachman and that Frenchie, who looked like a piece of soft bright velvet but had wrists of steel when it came to horses and who must be good in the field if those gold badges meant anything.

Three men rode along in front of him. One was Francis Levett, and John saw that he no longer hid the fact that he was a soldier but wore his bandolier and sword and carried a musket across his saddle. Two men in the road stopped talking and melted into the shadows of the inn and women shut windows, barring them as the men passed by, slowly, deliberately and with seeming contempt for all they saw. John turned aside into a lane that led beside the road and into the back of the Cathedral Close. He urged the mule faster and knocked on the back door of one of the main buildings. A guard opened it.

'There's armed men up to no good,' he said briefly. 'Get this inside the kitchen and bar the door in the outer wall after me. Tell the Governor to expect trouble, for Francis Levett would never come out in the open unless he had more men at his back to protect him. Send a man along the side roads to watch the road from Warwick and if he fires a shot, you'll know that the rumours are true and that Lord Brooke is bent on a fight.'

'Come in with us! We'll be safe inside the Close. The bridge is up and the doors are too stout to give way to a battering. We can defend the moat, and the King's men will be here to relieve us when they hear that we are in danger. I'll send word to Oxford and to Prince Rupert, and we can sweat it out if they surround the cathedral, but they will never broach these walls and it would be sacrilege to do harm to God's house.'

'You need more arms,' said John, alarmed at the complacency of the guard. 'You have but few guns and not much store of food as I recall, and too many idle mouths to feed who will be useless in battle.'

'There will be no battle. We are law-abiding and honest and have not taken arms against Oliver. Leastways, the ones remaining have nothing to fear and those who joined the Prince are far away. We have few horses left for an army to take and we shall need no stores once we parley with them. If they see that we depend on our fish and hens and have no great store of fodder they will go away. Parliament troops pass through most towns now and do no harm if the people stay quiet. They are the law-makers and not our enemy, and soon the King will return to Whitehall and life will go back to the old days.'

He called for servants to take the venison to a place of safety deep within the walls of the fortified church precincts and hurried to tell the Governor what John Levett had told him. Orders were given for men to be posted on rooftops with muskets along the way the troops would come, and John felt that the Governor had more sense than the minor canons who put their trust in the respect that they thought all men must have for the cathedral.

He went back the way he had come and in through the back door of the cottage, leaving the mule tied up with his own horse. 'Where's Lucy?' he asked.

'She went to work,' said her mother. 'There are brasses to be cleaned and she should have been there early before the services.'

John swore and then relaxed. 'She'll be as safe there as anywhere,' he said. He eyed Jane with anxiety. 'You worry me more.' He smelled the pungent mixture simmering on the fire and recalled Francis Turner and his hatred of the woman since she derided him in public and reminded him of his childhood, before he had the power to hurt and no means to bring fear to his old adversaries. He remembered the time he had fought Francis when he called Jane a witch and John knew the man had many old scores to settle.

A bell rang as the town crier called to the people of Lichfield to stay peaceable and allow the passage of the men loyal to the Lord Protector of England to pass through the city, and to make way for Lord Grenville Brooke who would be there within half a day.

He read from a stiff scroll. 'Hear ye, hear ye! There is no cause for anguish. Our Lord Protector brings peace and justice to all who obey Parliament and to honest folk, but beware those who worship idols and follow the Pope, all who fornicate, or are adulterers, and may all who practise witchcraft beware.'

'He speaks against the Church,' said Jane. 'We are not papists but they envy the rich trappings of the cathedral and the wealth of the Close. We worship the Lord and the cathedral sends praise to Him. The three spires are raised to Heaven, and if these wicked men touch a stone, they will be destroyed.'

'Lord Brooke is a fanatic who hates the Church,' said John. 'He has burned many who held the Eucharist and lets his men run amok on holy ground.' His face was pale. 'You must come away, Jane. If Lucy is within the Close, she will be safe and I shall come back to find her.'

'I must stay. If there is trouble, my herbs will help the wounded, and Lucy may come home and wonder where I am.'

'Tell your neighbour that you have been summoned to a sick woman in labour and that Lucy must manage until you return, then gather clothes and some vittals and load the mule while I get water and ale. Bring two warm cloaks and candles,' he added.

Jane did as he told her and was ready when he returned. 'Where are you taking me?' she asked. 'I have no relatives who would keep me.'

'Lady Hester will take you,' he said with conviction, 'but first you must hide for a few days in case they go to the manor and ask for you. I shall tell no one where you are until it is safe to go to my lady and to Hope, and I will look after Lucy.'

Jane forced a laugh as she looked back into her neat kitchen.

She had pulled the pot away from the fire and left it on the hearth. 'If they come here looking for witches, they can have that,' she said. 'It's a purge for old Mistress Bacon who is costive and needs gunpowder to shift her bowels, and the other in the dish is a poultice and not good to eat even if it does smell of wholesome linseed.' She saw the carcass of the deer on the big deal table. 'Lucy will grow fat,' she said. 'But what if men come here? They will rob us! Help me!' She dragged the cover off her bed in the dark inglenook. They heaved the unflayed carcass on to the bed and covered it with the sheet. 'Lucy will find it,' said Jane.

'We must hurry and go by way of the fields and woodland,' said John. He led the mule behind the horse that was big enough to carry two and they left Quonians Lane silently. Shutters were over windows and no man trod the streets and so they went unseen.

The ruined chapel was as he had left it, and there was no further sign of habitation. Jane watched as he pulled back the slab of stone and lit a candle. Her eyes widened but not with fear, as he took her down into the dry crypt. 'I never knew what was here,' she said. He brought bundles of straw to make a warm bed and pulled a big stone down the steps to make a table. He showed her the backdoor but warned her that the stinging nettles were shoulder high from the steps, and if she had to escape that way, she must wrap her face and arms in a cloak and push through, blind.

'I'll warn them at the manor that Lord Brooke is on his way to Lichfield and you must stay here. Hope knows about this place and she can come to fetch you if all is well, but you have food and water and candles to last for days.'

She saw that he was worried and took his hand in a rare gesture of tenderness. 'You are a good man, John, and I'm proud to have you as a son-in-law. Never think I shall be unhappy or afeared. I can sleep and think and save the candles for reading my Bible, and use the tomb in that alcove for shelter if anyone finds this place.' She smiled as she ran a hand over the heavy stone half-hidden in the shadows. 'I am not afraid of the dead. Only the living.'

'Take no heed if you hear noises,' he said. 'There were men here for a night, but they don't know of this crypt and they used the chapel only when they met Francis as spies. I shall put a pile of dust and pebbles over the slab and it will be as it has been for years.' Awkwardly, he kissed her cheek. 'I must go to the manor,' he said and she heard him rake stones and dust back over the slab of stone that made her a prisoner and yet also gave her freedom.

The groom looked up from the harness he was polishing and eyed John with surprise. 'I came back to look for a knife I lost,' John lied. 'And there is news from Lichfield that Lord Brooke is going into the city today.'

'We are not in his way,' said the groom. 'We are law-abiding and keep our thoughts to ourselves.'

'There is nothing to fear,' John agreed. 'But Lady Hester must hear the news and be ready in case they visit her.' He spoke carelessly as if it was not his concern, but he was secretly ashamed that he could no longer voice his own opinions. He saw, too, how cautious the man had become. Last week he had spoken for the King, and yet now he seemed to sit on the fence to await the fate of whichever side lost.

Lady Hester came into the Great Hall quickly, looking,

anxious. John noticed the curious stare of a servant and repeated his excuse that he had lost a knife, so the man went away. 'My lady,' John said in a low voice, 'Lord Brooke is on his way into Lichfield and there are many who will make this the time to harass their enemies. My Lucy is safe within the walls of the Close, but her mother is hated by Francis Turner and may be condemned as a witch.'

'Bring her here. No man dare touch a woman under my roof,' she said with pride. 'I have papers, which my husband left, that forbid any Parliamentarian to enter without my consent.' She gave a rueful smile. 'Sir Edwin has a nephew who travels with Lord Cromwell and has the power to protect us. A mealy-faced boy he was and yet now more powerful than we are in matters of state until the King returns to Whitehall.'

'I have hidden her until we know it is safe for her to come here. In these times, it is better to keep a still tongue unless we are sure of loyalty. One of your footmen comes from Lichfield and was a crony of Turner's and there may be others whom you cannot trust, my lady.'

'Where is Jane Willow?'

John shook his head. 'Hope knows where she is, but if you have no idea then you have no burden of lying, Lady Hester. I shall go back now and try to find out more. If the men pass through peaceably, then all will be well, but if they siege the cathedral, we may have to wait and keep low.' He saw the manservant enter the Hall. 'Did the stallion give any trouble, madam?'

'He kicked the straw, but settled,' she said. 'Monsieur Barill was much taken with him and hopes to buy him from my husband.'

'The French gentleman wears strange badges, my lady.' John's own curiosity was tinged with anxiety to know more about the man who had so obviously been attracted to Hope.

'He comes from good stock,' she said. 'A younger son, but with wealth enough, for any man, and vast estates in Burgundy and the Rhône valley in France. He will have no title but prefers to mix easily with his squires and horsemen as well as he does with the nobility.'

'He's a pretty man,' said John with a shrug.

'Handsome and strong,' said Lady Hester. 'He is unmarried and yet did nothing to make my maids cry or provoke him to lust, but he is a man.' She looked serious. 'He was much taken with Hope and she with him, John. I pray that nothing bad comes of it when he returns.' She opened her reticule. 'Hope found this after he left. He must miss it and think it gone forever.' She handed him the gold pin and John held it carefully while he tried to read the engraving. 'It says his name and that it was presented by the lord who owns the estates where the games took place. It gives him great honour,' she added.

'I can mend it. The clasp is loose and needs the touch of a hot iron to mould it into shape. Is the furnace hot?'

Lady Hester called the groom and gave the order to make a small furnace hot. 'There are trinkets of mine that need attention too, if your great hands can hold them,' she said, admiring the delicate way he took the pin and examined it. 'Do these things for me and then eat dinner with Hope and confide what you have said to me.'

Hope tried to hide her dismay when he told her the news and made him hurry over his dinner to get back to Lichfield.

'Tell no one,' he warned her. 'I trust only a few now that the country is in fear. Only you and Lady Hester and I must know where Jane is now.' For the fifth time he explained that Jane was warm, safe and had plenty of food and drink to last for several days and that he would bring her as soon as possible to the comfort of the manor.

Without the heavily laden mule, John rode fast and took quiet roads, coming into Lichfield at the back of Quonians Lane. He heard shouting and looked towards the cathedral. Armed men stood in line below the walls, and the crier was made to read another proclamation urging the Governor to leave the Close and give himself up so that Lord Brooke could enter the cathedral. John went to his own cottage but it was empty. More heavy boots marched into the square and horses dragged guns that now pointed towards the spires. The local people stayed indoors and peeped through cracks in their shutters; only men in the sober garb of the Puritans went out to watch.

Sam Levett stood by a small group of soldiers and looked pleased with himself. He looked towards the cottages as if to see some sign of life in Jane's cottage, and said something to a man who laughed and looked back as well. John recognized Francis Turner and wondered if he could keep his fists to himself but was thankful that Lucy was safe. A cart piled with goods taken from shops on the way into the city was pushed up to the doorway of a handsome house by the market, and a protesting apothecary had to watch while his house was taken over for the use of officers. No violence occurred and the men waited as if for orders. There was even a certain reluctance among them, many of whom came from the county and had come into the city for market days and festivals and had grown up with the beautiful silhouette of the cathedral on the skyline. There was reverence for the church and a superstitious belief that God would strike any who desecrated His house, so they waited for Lord Brooke to arrive and show them what to do. With him they might have more courage to attack the church, as he had harangued his troops with the ardent message that he would want to be struck dead if he wasn't in the right to persecute the unrighteous and to hound the wicked.

Dusk fell and more men and arms came with tents and the requisitioning of barns and halls to house the soldiers. John slept well, almost guiltily as he knew that no soldier would take the cottage of Sam Levett who was faithful to the cause of Cromwell, and the Turners would be safe, but in the early hours near dawn he heard footsteps stop by Jane Willow's home and rough voices calling for her.

'Come out, you spawn of the devil,' they shouted. 'Lord Brooke will want an example made of people such as you. He comes tomorrow and will see a pretty burning by the moat where everyone can know what happens to those against Parliament and those who practise witchcraft.'

John watched through a slit in the blind and smiled grimly. 'You may look your fill,' he murmured.

The first soldier knocked on the door again, then kicked it, and it swung open as it wasn't bolted. The men drew back as if they thought that a witch would have barricaded herself in and have to be brought out by force. One man crossed himself then looked fearfully at his companions as this smacked of popery, but they seemed not to notice. Francis Turner stepped into the kitchen and paused. The fire was out and the room cold, and the poultice lay stiff on the hob. He picked up the black pot and sniffed at the contents. Old Mistress Bacon's purge had congealed in the bottom of the pot and when Francis put a finger in it and tasted it, he shuddered and spat on the floor.

'Witches' brew,' said the third man, looking scared. He backed away but Francis seized his arm and drew him further into the house.

'Come, Joseph, we are stronger than witches, and must make sure she has the signs. Jane Willow! Come out and be judged,' he called. He gave the coarse laugh of a man whose courage had been strengthened by strong waters. 'We shall see if you carry the third nipple, the mark of the Devil.' His eyes became accustomed to the lack of light and he saw the mound in the bed beside the fireplace. 'It's no use pretending to be asleep or dead,' he shouted. 'Joseph, drag her from her sty and strip her so that we may see the signs.'

Fearfully, and inwardly saying a forbidden Hail Mary, the simple soldier raised the bottom of the sheet, then screamed and fell back, struggling to get past the other two men and out into the holier air. 'The cloven hoof!' he shrieked. 'It is the Devil.'

Francis restrained him with difficulty, his own courage seeping away. 'What saw you?'

'Cloven hooves and a hairy leg like the pagan gods.' He tore himself free and ran from the cottage, and the other two followed without waiting to see what was under the sheet, but within the hour the news had spread that Jane Willow had been taken by the Devil and had left his image in her bed.

People came to look at the open door of the cottage, but none dared venture inside. John waited until the attention of the crowd was diverted by the noise of marching feet and the sound of drums, and slipped in through the back door to take the venison to the stable at the back of his own home where he flayed the meat, discarded the skin and cut the joints ready to hang and grow tender.

Many simple men who had doubted the justice and wisdom of Parliament were now convinced that they fought evil and they thrust down feelings of traditional loyalty to the throne.

John went back to Jane's cottage and stood by the open doorway. Francis Turner saw him and came back, bringing two other soldiers, angry that John Levett should stand so calmly where he had fled. 'We shall see now what's here now that we have left that craven clod with the women,' he said, as if Joseph had needed any help in leaving the cottage.

John stood aside, smiling while the sheet was lifted from the bed and no body of Jane, the Devil or of his minion was found. 'Is something wrong?' he asked.

'Did you see aught?' asked one of the soldiers. 'Some say they saw her rise on a broomstick and fly away.'

'And some say they saw the Devil take her naked on his back,' said the other.

Francis looked furious as he realized that somehow he'd been tricked. He examined the bed more closely and saw the marks made from the seeping blood and juices from the carcass. 'She had carnal intercourse with the Devil and he took her for his own,' he said, with more conviction than he felt. 'We must search for her and bring her to the fire.'

'She may be in the cathedral,' said one.

'Not if she's with the Devil,' said the other. He lost interest and told the others that the troops were gathering for inspection. Lord Brooke was expected now that the guns were assembled, pointing towards the cathedral spires. Once more the crier called for the doors of the Close to be opened, and once again the Governor refused to give access to a holy place.

Horsemen came from the main road and into the square and in the fore was Lord Grenville, resplendent in full armour. He rode to the house which had been taken for him and went inside, leaving his followers to make their presence felt in the city and to give time for the townsfolk to be intimidated into acceptance of his power. Guns were trained on the gate from Dam Street into the Close, but in spite of the city putting up no opposition, the Cathedral Close remained sealed and the Earl of Chesterfield, Governor of the City, refused to budge.

Eyes behind shutters and in dark corners watched as preparations were made to attack the gate, and Lord Brooke walked from his dwelling in the market square, along the narrow passages to Dam Street so that he could be there when the first shots were fired. In the cold spring breeze, he raised his visor to see better and the sun glinted on the gilded bars of the steel helmet.

A man on a roof saw the glint of gold and it made a fine marker for his shot. Almost carelessly, the bullet passed beyond the gold and steel into the brain of the fanatical commander of Cromwell's invading force, and he fell dead before the gate that he had come to see shattered. A groan went up from the ranks and was echoed by the townsfolk, with murmurings of God's vengeance and His retribution for blasphemy.

The body was dragged back through the lanes and the captain in charge of the guns gave the order to fire, before too many people recalled Lord Brooke's boast that he hoped he would be struck down if his cause was not just.

More men were brought from Derby and Coventry and a new commander with no truck with superstition took over, attacking the Close and the city centre.

'The King's army must be told,' it was murmured in places where men trusted each other, and messages were sent at night to alert the forces in Tamworth; however they were but a flea bite on the neck of a lion and could not deflect the Roundheads.

Citizens watched helplessly, pressed back by armed men, when women and children were seized and used as a human barrier to allow the Roundheads to get closer to their goal. Lichfield was torn as it had never been, by fire and mixed ideals and the devastation of the grenades filled with gunpowder. John saw the market cross crumble in a heap of rubble and many fine houses fall before the guns. The saintly spires remained whole and defiant but at last, a few days after the first attack, the Governor parleyed for a truce and gave up the Close and the cathedral to Sir John Gell, the new commander.

'So much destroyed in such a short while,' said Meg Turner. She came from the safety of the Close where she had been working when the drawbridge had been shut and the portcullis lowered, and now hardly spoke to her son. Her hair was whiter than it had been a week ago and her face showed all the signs of strain and humiliation that she felt by having a son like Francis.

'You'll lack for nothing, Mother,' he said. 'We have taken the stronghold and it's packed with riches, and ours for the taking.'

'Riches?' she said with a rarely seen burst of spirit. 'What riches when all my friends look at me as if I were dirt?'

'You should be proud to have a son ready to stand up for what is right and just, and who fights for the downfall of the men who have been our masters for too long. We fish and hunt now with no fear of hanging, and the silver from the churches will bring arms and food for our Lord Protector's men.'

She looked at the fine carp he threw on the table, taken that morning from the minster pool, and pushed it to one side. 'We have better than fish,' she said. 'John Levett brought me deer liver and some venison to hang or smoke.' She smiled and Francis lowered his gaze before her derision. 'Everyone in Lichfield knows about that,' she said. 'Joseph Martin mistaking a deer for the Devil! And rightly-gained deer at that, given by Sir Edwin himself to repay John for farrier work.'

'I'll throw it in the pond,' Francis threatened.

'No, you won't. You'll build a smoking shed out of the bricks lying by the ruins that your men have made, and we'll have a store of meat against the time when the tide turns and the other army comes here.' She gave a tired sigh. 'Oh, they'll come and go, and come and go until this sorry squabble is over and the court is back in London, and whoever wins it won't be us.'

She reached for the huge fish and a gutting knife. 'We'll smoke fish, too, while they allow you to catch it.' She looked at him shrewdly. 'They'll give you leave to do this for as long as it suits them, and after that you'll be hanged for it, but in the name of Cromwell this time. Thieving gets its reward under any banner once law and order are restored, and one of the soldiers said that Cromwell had punished some of his own men for rape and for being too zealous with a gun or knife.'

'His commanders take a different view. They burn witches,' Francis said, as if to convince himself.

'They try them first, even if it is only by the ordeal of water, and they have use for women with the skill of healing. The wounds of all men stink in time if not tended and they need women who can make them sweet, so be careful who you burn, my son.'

# V

Lady Hester Clinton looked across the meadows to the barns where last year's hay and grain were stored. Men now slept in the barns to protect them, and as yet no thieving had reached the manor as she had made a bold show of the documents giving her protection from injury or loss. Grain sacks filled a cart ready to go to the mill, and men with cudgels walked beside it to bring back the milled flour. The fact that she had been forced to concede some grain to the new commander in Lichfield made her sigh, but it was a small price to pay for immunity and the house was far enough from the main roads to be hidden now that the leafy trees made a dense shield.

The distant silhouettes of horses and men working the land gave the lie to the turmoil in the city, and many of the families in the cottages had not heard a shot fired. She turned to ride back but first urged her horse to the rise where she could see the road to Oxford.

'Come, Hope,' she called and Hope bit her lip and cautiously pressed the flanks of the pony she was learning to ride, hoping it wouldn't break into the terrifying trot that had brought her over the rough field.

The road was as empty as it had been each time they had come here to look for any sign of Sir Edwin returning. 'No word and only rumours,' said Lady Hester.

'It is but six or seven weeks since they left, my lady,' said Hope, now more confident with her pony standing still and the ground even, but the pony wanted to crop the young spring grass and bent his head suddenly, making Hope cling to the reins. She pulled his head up as the groom had taught her and was pleased that she was becoming more proficient. They rode back slowly, enjoying the sight of new growth and the hedgerows full of primroses and violets.

It was so quiet that it was difficult to imagine Lichfield with its noise and the clatter of armour and horses' hooves, the occasional scuffle and the atmosphere of despair in many of the once-prosperous houses. With the Roundheads firmly in command and the battered Close made fast again, it looked as if Parliament could add Lichfield to its tally of subdued towns.

'Come, Hope, we must go back and make sure that Abbie has food enough prepared should Sir Edwin return today or tomorrow.'

Hope glanced at her mistress and was saddened to see the new lines on the lovely face and the almost too slender waist. 'He'll come back soon, my lady,' she said, softly. 'They'll all come back.' She thought of the elaborate gold brooch that the Frenchman had left behind, and her pulse quickened. He must come back to find it, and maybe this time she wouldn't act like a stupid child, dragging her hand away from his kiss as if his lips had stung instead of complimented her.

Hester looked down to the manor house, and its beauty and mellow age made her catch her breath as if seeing it for the first time. For how long would they live in peace? If the army grew impatient and lacked food and cattle, would this place ever be as it had been when she first came here as a bride, and would signatures on documents protect them forever? 'Was Jane content this morning?' she asked.

Hope smiled. 'Content and grateful, my lady. She says she owes her life to you.'

'To John Levett and you, Hope. She merely sleeps beneath my roof and pays her way by making soft unguents and salves that I can get in no other place now. I do not think they'll look for her here again.'

'John was right to make her stay hidden for so long,' said Hope. She shuddered, recalling the morning when at first light the maids were taking out ashes to the midden and the men were opening the stables, and men had come wearing the uniform of the Parliamentarian army. One went to the stables and one to the kitchen without a *by-your-leave, my lady* to ask the servants if they harboured a witch. The other had demanded to see Lady Hester. Hope smiled faintly, remembering the impatience of the non-commissioned officer who first strutted by the empty fireplace in the Hall and then stood by the window looking more subdued, until Lady Hester summoned him to her small sitting-room.

'A witch? Here?' Lady Hester laughed. 'And this not even the full moon! Was she seen in the sky over our house riding the wind?'

The soldier looked uncomfortable. 'Her name is Willow, my lady, Mistress Willow.'

'Willow?' Lady Hester picked up a book from the small table and fingered the gold tooled leather of the cover. 'I know the name.'

'Yes, my lady?' he prompted eagerly.

'Lucy Willow is the friend of my companion Hope Levett, who is the sister of John Levett, the farrier to whom I hear Lucy Willow is now betrothed. I cannot think her a witch, with all those honest connections. You have two Levetts in your ranks, I believe.'

'That is so,' he replied, with ebbing confidence.

'So Lucy is almost related to them and so commands your protection.'

'We have no quarrel with Miss Lucy. It is Jane Willow we seek.'

'Why here? I can think of no time when she was here, unless to visit the kitchen and Abbie would remember if she had come for any reason, but I believe that your men have already taken the liberty of going there uninvited to ask her.'

The man shuffled uneasily. 'We were told she might be here.'

Lady Hester turned away to hide a smile. 'Look in her cottage. She is there, feasting on the venison that my husband gave to John Levett. He is a good man and I'm sure he gave her a share, as she is the mother of his intended bride.'

The officer reddened even more. Sam and Francis Levett had been the laughing stock of the platoon when they heard the tale of the venison and the devil's cloven hoof, but Francis had sworn he had proof that Jane Willow was a witch and so they had to try to find her, even if most of the men had no stomach for witch-baiting.

Hester went to the small bureau and raised the carved lid. 'I have ordered draughts of sack for you and your men, and I ask you to look anywhere you like within these estates and then go. You may search for witches, warlocks or escaped hens if it pleases you, but once only, and never come here again or I shall write to your commander and quote from these papers. My husband has a diplomatic right to live here, and to fill his house with whomever he wishes, and to pass freely between the King and Parliament. You have disobeyed this order and should suffer for it, but I will take your word that we shall not be troubled by you again on such a flimsy pretext.' Her smile was almost kind and understanding. 'You are an honest man and these are bad times, but peace will come and it is as well to know our friends. Your voice tells me that you are from this county.'

'From Elford, my lady.'

She regarded him with amusement. 'You have the look of the Huddlestones about you. Did your grandmother do more than fish for eels on a fine night down by the river?'

'They do say summat, my lady.'

'Then we may be kin!' she said gaily. 'Look in the gallery. We have portraits of de Aldernes, Stanleys and Huddlestones, and you may see a likeness.' She walked him past the old portraits and made sure that he found one that she swore had his likeness. Hester laughed softly when he left to drink the good sack that Abbie had for him and to collect his men and remove them from her sight. An extra jauntiness in his step showed his pride in the new belief that he had aristocratic blood in his sluggish veins, and a disloyal sense of protection for Lady Hester and her family.

And now, Jane was safe in the attic room that once Hope had occupied, and ventured out only after dark to take the air, with Hope taking her food and Dorcas keeping her company when she could take her sewing there. She was trying to learn something about the lore of herbs, and Jane agreed to teach her.

Lady Hester called the groom and Hope dismounted, thankfully. 'The second footman ran off this morning,' said George. 'Said he'd do more good in the army, and we're glad to see the back of him. That is, if you can manage without him, my lady.' He took both bridles to lead the horses away.

'Was that all he said?' asked Hope.

'He was tired of finding out nowt, if you ask me. Always coming up soft behind us and listening, he must have been disappointed not to find Royalists under the beds.' He gave Lady Hester a keen look. 'A lot safer without him, and I'm sure there's no more of his ilk left here. We all take what comes, my lady, and wish no harm to anyone.'

Hope took off her riding cloak and fetched a pot of pure lanolin, boiled from sheep's wool and skimmed clean, from the kitchen. She put it in the basket with the pile of primroses and violets she had gathered that morning and ran up the back stairs to Jane. 'Can you make anything of these?' she asked. 'They are not so strong as roses or lilies but they have a sweet scent.'

Jane smiled. 'I shall boil some now with roots to seal the scent, and the others will lie in the fat for a week or so and then be pressed. It will make a salve for her ladyship, and some for you if you want smooth hands like a lady.' She looked less pale, Hope noticed with relief. The week she had spent in almost total darkness had taken its toll on her colour and she had emerged from the crypt like a plant deprived of light.

'Leave your things,' John had whispered, the night he came

to release her. He put six candles on the makeshift table and fresh water in the keg.

'You think I might have to come back?' Jane asked fearfully.

'It might be any of us,' he replied darkly. 'It's as well to know of this place.'

Jane opened the door at the back of the crypt a little and threw out the remains of the food. 'I want no rats in here if I have to come back,' she said. 'I put my ordure outside to keep the room sweet and the door is still hidden by the nettles.'

He helped her out and carefully covered the stone slab again before half lifting her on to the nag and leading it from the ruins, back to a bed and hot food for Jane and the care of Lady Hester and Hope.

'They have given up looking for Jane,' John told them. 'The sergeant who came here swears that there is no sign of her, and that she was last seen flying away towards Abbot's Bromley. They leave Lucy in peace, but she will be safer married to me, so we will wed next week in Alrewas, where they still give a blessing decently and not as Lord Brooke decreed, that folk should marry before a justice with no blessing of the Church.'

'He's dead, so he can do you no harm,' said Hope. 'It's plain what Heaven thought of him. He was struck down when he ordered the cathedral to be attacked.'

'The new commander is as harsh, and it will be good to live with Lucy and keep a place warm for Jane when times are better.'

'It is sad that Jane cannot come to your wedding,' said Hope.

'You will come as a witness?' he asked anxiously. 'It's better if we keep away from here that day and have our dinner in the inn close by the church in Alrewas.'

'I shall ride with you,' Hope said proudly. 'Lady Hester will let me take the pony, and I am good in the saddle now.'

'Wear nothing bright to attract attention,' John warned. 'Lucy must seem to be in mourning for her mother as well as joyful to be wed, and the less people talk, the better.'

Hope pressed a dark dress but added lace to the throat and took a pretty shawl to wear over her hair in church. Lichfield seemed far away and she was pensive as she waited for the day of the wedding to come, wondering if anything could prevent the marriage, but, at last, she was waiting with her pony by the slab of stone used as a mounting block. Lady Hester grew paler each day because news of the war was bad in other parts of the country and there was no news of her husband, and the little party set off soberly to Alrewas.

'We can have no music,' the cleric said, 'and I must read the service quickly.' He looked defiant. 'But I will give you the blessing of the Church and you will know that you are married in the sight of God.'

'The birds make enough music,' said Lucy, looking up into the good face of the man she was about to marry. 'I need no dancing or revelry, sir. I am thankful for a good man and cottage with a hearth where we may live.'

'You have no other family?'

'My father is with the Roundheads, and Lucy has no father now. Her mother has left the city for safety,' John interposed quickly. 'This is my sister who is companion to Lady Hester Clinton.'

'My regards to her ladyship, and I pray for Sir Edwin on his dangerous travels between the Court and Parliament. I hear that many carts of goods from France that came through the

northern ports have fallen to Cromwell on the way to Oxford.'
He sighed. 'Now that Lichfield has fallen, goods must travel
far round the city to get to the King, and I can't see the day
when Parliament will give up this valuable fortified link
between north and south.' He hesitated. 'This is your joyful
day, but may I beg a favour?' John nodded. 'My son is a master
at the grammar school and I long for news of him. With
theatres closed, ale houses shut and the cathedral desecrated,
I fear for the schools.'

'He is safe, sir. They leave the schools alone if the masters
teach no religion, and I can take a letter to him if you wish it,
and bring a reply when I come next to Alrewas.'

'I once regretted that my son didn't follow me but wanted
only to teach the Classics, and now I praise God in His
wisdom that my son does nothing to offend Parliament.' The
old man ushered them into the nave and up to the altar. 'Let
us raise our hearts to the Lord!' he said, and while the birds
sang on the blossom sprays of the pear trees, and Hope
dreamed of a man with a velvet hat and a bold glance, John
and Lucy were joined in holy matrimony.

The well-cooked fowl and cured ham made a dinner worthy
of the day, and the cleric joined them with two more men with
whom John had worked in a farm forge. They talked of the old
days and the dim future but not of Lichfield and the army in
control there, as now everyone distrusted strangers and there
were some at other tables in the inn.

'You should come here when we have the maypole. You
could dance for your wedding then, and it's only a week or so
away, is Mayday,' said one of the men.

'They'll wait for the dancing for a long while,' said his

companion drily. 'They cut it down and said it was wicked and pagan and not fit for honest folk, and if this inn wasn't convenient for the troops passing, they'd shut this too. He winked and lowered his voice. 'We brew our own ale and have a cockpit behind the barn that we cover if strangers come nosing. They can't expect men to give up everything just to please a man with a face like a yard of pump water.'

'He promises better times for such as we, with better pay than six pounds a year and a tied cottage.'

'And nothing to spend it on? No inns, no cockfights, no baiting, no theatres and whores?'

'And no freedom if you talk so loud,' said John as he saw two soldiers enter the inn. Lucy turned pale and begged to be taken back to the familiar safety of her own cottage, and Hope was glad when they were once more on the way to the manor. Lucy had to be kissed by all the servants and by Lady Hester, who gave her a bedsheet with lace ends and a cloth to cover the deal kitchen table on high days and holidays.

'I'll ride with you to the road,' said Hope, who was proud of her mastery over the pony. 'And then I must see to Lady Hester's clothes and dress her hair.'

Laughing, they said goodbye but when Hope waved from the edge of the coppice by the lodge she was sad, envying their happiness and knowing that she must return to see the tragedy in the eyes of her mistress. A sound made her turn and she heard hoofbeats on the hard road. She remembered the soldiers in the inn who had eyed her with open lust and might have followed the party. There had been tales of local girls caught and raped who dared not point a finger at their tormentors.

With a sudden jerk of the reins, she turned the pony. He took fright from her own panic and bolted, jerking the reins from her hand, and the world dissolved into whirling blackness as she was thrown heavily to the ground.

Hope became aware of men and horses, and of strong arms that lifted her carefully and carried her on to a wattle hurdle. Her eyes were closed and the movement over rough ground made her wince but she couldn't locate the pain. It was everywhere, as if she had been shaken like the dice the Roundheads said were the Devil's own, and thrown into a pit of rocks.

Dreams like white mist came and went, and she thought she smelled perfume as she was lifted once more on to a softer couch than the uneven wattle. Her eyelids fluttered. Perfume? She tried to bring her mind back, but it couldn't be held firm and she drifted off into a another dream.

'She lives.' A woman spoke as if in contempt of all the concern that had come with the girl to the house.

'Some strong waters and a good slap,' suggested the voice she now recognized as Abbie's.

'*Non*! Not now,' said a voice that Hope had wondered if she would ever hear again. 'See, her heart flutters and her pulse is weak.' Hope felt a firm hand over her breast and a compress of cold water on her brow. She stirred and pulled away from the cold, wet cloth. The hand on her breast seemed now to be more of a caress.

The acrid smell of burned feathers and aromatic herbs made her cough and take deep breaths. 'Now a little eau de vie,' said Jerard Barill. 'Thank you, Madame. I shall thank you for a supply of those salts. It would wake the dead!'

Hope opened her eyes and saw a circle of faces over the bed

in the room close to Lady Hester's that was now hers. Jane Willow held the reviving salts under Hope's nose again and she waved them away as she coughed and caught her breath sharply, but when she tried to move, she realized that she ached all over and that there was blood on her hands. Lady Hester held her husband by the hand and her face was radiant now that Edwin was home and she knew that Hope was not dying.

Jane smiled and told her to stay still until she had seen where the hurt was, and Jerard Barill knelt by the bed with such an expression of concern on his handsome face that Hope blushed and her heart beat faster and more strongly. He took one of her hands, tenderly. The torn fingernails and one deep scratch covered with congealed blood seemed not to matter as he gently kissed the dirty palm.

Abbie grunted. 'You don't get that at a farthing a bottle,' she said and went down to the kitchen to tell the kitchen maids that Mistress Hope was alive, lying there like a lady and making the most of her fall to enchant the handsome Frenchman, and that Jane Willow had appeared as if by magic.

'Did she fly in on a broomstick?' asked one of the maids fearfully.

'She's been here with Lady Hester,' said Dorcas. 'And now that Sir Edwin's back she can come out and show herself, as he will protect her.'

Abbie sent up warm ale and a bowl of gruel, and Jane asked for hot water and fresh linen. Lady Hester led away all but Jane and one maid and called for food for the returning men.

'I shall wash away the dust first, Madame,' Jerard said. His valet went to fetch warm water, then shaved his master's cheeks and trimmed the short beard before Barill stripped and washed his body in scented water and applied pomade to his hair and beard as though he were about to meet someone important. He slapped the dust from his hat, removed the gold pin in the shape of a gun and fixed it to his tunic. He paused as he passed the doorway to Hope's room, seeing that the door was open slightly. He pushed it further open and stepped inside, then stopped. Jane was bending over the girl's nearly naked body, applying a warm salve to the many bruises on her arms and legs and stomach. Hope's cut hands were swathed in strips of linen steeped in St John's wort and alkanet to soothe the pain and to heal the small wounds, although the dye of the alkanet made them look even redder than when the blood flowed, so she was glad to have them covered.

Jerard drew in his breath sharply. The exquisite lines of the girl's body made him feel the lust harden in his loins, but her air of innocent vulnerability and trust added an unfamiliar dimension to his feelings. Of the women he had bedded, never scullery maids or their like, but pretty women and girls of some rank, he had never wanted to sit by them merely to hold a hand or soothe a brow with gentle kisses.

Jane glanced towards the door and smiled, then drew the sheet modestly over the girl's thighs. 'She is *très belle*,' he whispered. 'So beautiful.'

'And good,' Jane said with slight reproach. She walked towards him and spoke softly so that Hope could not hear. 'She has good blood and little dross in her veins and deserves a husband and rank, not men who will take her and use her and leave her as her mother was used.' Her steady grey eyes made him lower his own gaze. 'Go and eat, sir. You are not needed here.'

He touched the gold brooch as if to convince himself of his own importance and backed away, only slightly resenting Jane's familiar tone and the implication that he was bent on seduction, and when Lady Hester met him and presented him with his other pin, mended and cleaned, he forgot the girl on the bed and took pride in telling the company how he had won the gold pins.

# VI

'Prince Rupert has reached Birmingham,' said Sir Edwin Clinton, quietly, as soon as he was alone with his wife that night.

Hester turned pale. 'Does that mean even more fighting? Will he come this way?'

'To Lichfield for certain, to take back the cathedral and to mend the desecration of the church,' he replied sternly. 'I met Lord Cromwell and I think he deplores the actions of many in his following, but there are those within his ranks who consider only force and the destruction of all order to be the aim of the army, and don't pursue his creed of law and order and the levelling of all men under his protection. He is as hard a man as I have met, and set against the divine right of the King and the power of the Church, but many of his new laws have reason behind them and could do good for the country, if the King would accept them.'

'His Majesty must be brought back to Westminster,' said Hester. 'London is a sorry place by all accounts, with people solemn and afeared and all amusements stopped. Even the innocent dancing of the morris men may not be watched, or so

I hear, and that reaches out to all the towns and villages where Cromwell has marched.'

'The King has many debts, and even now, in Oxford where he is loved, there are murmurings that his army expects too much credit for goods, and that they don't cut their cloth according to what they can afford.' He sighed. 'It was ever so. Men in danger and suffering loss of standing often drink too much and indulge in profligacy, drowning their thoughts of the future and taking solace in the company of whores and villains who fawn on the King and tell him that all will be well.'

'Will it be so? Will the King come back to his own, and shall we forget this terrible time?' Lady Hester begged as if her husband could arrange the future as she desired it to be.

'No, madam. We must face events as they occur and say little if we are to sleep easy in our beds. I exchanged letters between the Protector and King Charles, but I shall stay here while any action is taken that could make me less neutral, and you must show no preference to either side.'

'Not even when soldiers come searching for witches, sir?'

Edwin frowned. 'They wouldn't dare,' he said.

'Then you must stay at home and make sure they dare not do so again!' she retorted. 'They came here and harangued the servants about Jane Willow, who is now under our protection although she was not here when the soldiers came.' Hester smiled faintly. 'Partly through fear of your papers of safe passage and partly because I charmed the sergeant, I doubt if they'll come back.' She saw his anger and put a hand on his arm. 'Smile, Edwin! I know they will not return now, and Jane's daughter Lucy has married John Levett whose father is strong for Cromwell, and that must protect Lucy and her mother now.'

'If Jane is here, she can be useful. Two of my men were with the King and were wounded. They fester and need such things as she can prepare, and we must make sure that she has all she needs in case of more wounded who find a way here.'

'From Lichfield?'

He nodded. 'The King's army marches even now, and they have strong support from the miners from Cannock as well as the Royalists.'

'I must call for Hope Levett to brush my hair,' said Hester, then shrugged. 'I forget that she is sick, but I depend on her more and more.' She told him of the events of the time when he had been away and they talked of the riding accident that had covered Hope with bruises.

'She learns to ride as a lady?' he asked, amused.

'She is a lady in all but name. Sam Levett never sired such a girl,' said Hester firmly, 'and her mother was a result of a union far above the man who married her grandmother.'

'*Le droit de seigneur*?' Edwin smiled. 'We have given up that amusing custom,' he said. 'Country girls with thick ankles, red faces and the smell of the sty were no great stimulation to lust.'

'But Hope Levett would be,' said Hester quietly. 'And if the tide goes for the King, I fear that she may be ill-used by men used to taking girls and deflowering them in idle pleasuring. With a name like Levett she would be taken as one of their breed, as bad as Sam Levett, and might carry the taint of Francis Turner who vows he has been promised her.'

'Do you want to make her your ward?' asked Edwin, and Hester nodded. 'Because of Francis Turner? She can refuse him and we can see that he does her no mischief. That is no good reason for such a gesture.'

Hester began to take the pins from her hair and picked up a hairbrush. 'Not for fear of Francis Turner,' she said. 'We have danger closer to home. Young Jerard Barill is taken with the girl and has the charm of an angel and the subtlety of the snake in Eden.'

'He is a fighting man in spite of the scented pomade,' said Edwin. 'He seems not to dally with maids or to waste time away from the chase or horses.'

'He paced the gallery by her door today and offered help to lift her down to a couch or to put her in a chair, and before the sun set, he brought her flowers from the woods,' Hester laughed. 'Is that your fighting man?'

'He is used to the tricks of diplomacy,' said Edwin. 'He is French and from the Court there, with letters of credit and influence that our son Charles has found useful in his journeys. Tomorrow, he goes into Lichfield with a few men to take letters to the Governor who is imprisoned in Lichfield House with many other wretched men, and he has other letters for the new Commander of Cromwell's contingent.' He laughed and unbelted his tunic. 'I told him to dress like a sober diplomat and not a popinjay, or they'll shoot him on sight.' Hester put down her hairbrush and held out her arms to him. 'Yes, my love,' he said. 'Come to bed. I have been away for too long.'

'You shall have your ward,' he whispered later when they lay in the darkness, close and drained of passion. 'Young blood is hot and she will need to be wed and not spoiled.'

Hester raised her head. 'Listen!'

Edwin went to the window and opened the shutters to the pearl haze before dawn. 'It is Barill,' he said. 'He rides my stallion and is dressed for Lichfield.'

'So early?'

'It has to be early,' said Edwin grimly. 'I want the letters delivered and the boy back here before the army arrives and he is caught between the fire.' He grunted. 'He wears a sober suit, but sports his velvet hat. I can see the gold pins from here, now safe on his tunic as he is afraid of losing one again.'

The horse stopped below the window and Jerard doffed his hat and bowed. His eyes sparkled and his cheeks were pink with elation and exertion. 'A fine beast, Monsieur. I like him and he rides well. May I take him this morning? My own beast is lame and the groom wants to blister him.'

'God go with you, my boy,' shouted Edwin. 'The men are ready with fresh horses, too?'

'*Bien sûr*. We shall be back for dinner with Lady Hester. I take six men.'

'Take care of your badges. The sight of gold makes men envious,' Edwin warned him.

Jerard laughed. 'They are *mon bon chance*, my good luck. I shall visit the man who mended them well and bring you news of your friends.'

'No! Give the letters and come away, Jerard. Stay no longer than you need.'

Jerard cupped one ear with his hand and grinned. '*Qu'est-ce que c'est? Je ne comprends pas.*' He wheeled the stallion in a flash of dark silk and power, and called to the men who waited by the stables. They set off at a gallop, and there was envy in the eyes of the older man, but as soon as they reached the spinney and the way to Lichfield, he shouted to his men to walk the horses and to gather closer.

They rode in almost total silence, the men yawning and grumbling at the early hour, but Jerard watched the road and the distant spires and wished he had ten men instead of six. He shifted the weight of his musket across his knees and checked the catches of his hand guns, then thrust them out of sight so that the small party would seem to offer no threat. The polished leather of one saddlebag hid the crossbow that travelled with him wherever he went, and the other had enough bolts to frighten a platoon and put extra weight on the horse to calm his spirit.

At first, the fields that they passed, which belonged to the Clinton estate, were lush with green shoots where the winter-sown wheat and oats grew undisturbed, the woods were well pollarded, and the sheep ran with new lambs at the approach of the sound of hooves. The sky brightened into dawn, and smoke from cottage chimneys rose as straight towards Heaven as the 'Ladies of the Vale', the three spires of the cathedral that now dominated the distance.

They rode on, and one of the men who had his origins in Whittington cursed as he saw familiar farms with untended fields and empty barns. No smoke came from the chimneys of two usually busy farmhouses, and the stable doors hung loose on plundered stalls. 'They took the farmer to Lichfield Gaol, and his family scattered to relatives out near Burton. They thieved all he had because someone denounced him as a Royalist, and some say he is dead.'

'It is sad, my friend,' said Jerard Barill, 'but today we are not visiting Lichfield in anger, but in diplomacy. There will be no sorties to the gaol to rescue friends, although you can use the time to find out where they are and how they fare.'

'They may take us, too,' said Wyatt.

'I think not. I have papers, and if they can't read, then we have our own friends with us, *n'est-ce pas*?' Jerard patted the musket across his saddle. 'Tell me where John Levett lives. I must see him before I return to Sir Edwin.'

'Then you walk into a Roundhead domain,' said Wyatt.

'I think not. Lady Hester told me that he is now married to the daughter of Jane Willow, and lives in their cottage. I wish to make him aware of what may happen soon and to tell him to keep a cool head.' He rode on in silence, his mind filled with the memory of the girl who was a Levett but surely not of their blood. He thought briefly of the girl his family had chosen for him to marry soon in France, and wondered how he had ever accepted their choice so flippantly, taking it for granted that she would serve as mother to his heirs and he could take his pleasure in other beds.

'*Allons!*' he shouted as they reached the outskirts of the city. 'Keep close and ride slowly behind me.' He straightened the small pennant bearing the flag of France and his own coat of arms, which swayed between the ears of the stallion, then sat proudly erect in the saddle, his gloved hand cold under the velvet as he controlled his mount with seemingly little effort.

The streets were deserted except for three women with buckets who braved the grey threat of guards to fetch water from the pumps and the conduit. They were all old and none of the soldiers gave them a second glance, but lounged in boredom with their muskets resting against the wall of the gaol that had once been a rich house.

A sergeant buttoned his tunic more tidily and stood in the way of the horses. Jerard handed him the letter that would take him to the Commander, and hoped that the man was literate. The soldier passed a hand over his badly shaved chin and nodded reluctantly. 'Three men only,' he said. He eyed the good horses with speculation. 'The rest can dismount and leave their nags by the water trough.'

Jerard shook his head. 'They carry gifts from Sir Edwin Clinton and must come with me,' he said firmly. He shot a glance at Wyatt who had brought up sharply beside him and was tense with controlled aggression. '*All* of us,' Jerard stressed, and the man stood back to let them go to the Close where the army had its headquarters. There, Jerard detailed one man to look after the horses in a side alley where he could, if necessary, fight off any who might think of taking them, and called to the officer of the guard.

A man dressed in dark grey fustian and a steel breastplate bade him enter a small room that was part of the thick wall of the Close. Through the narrow window at the back of the room, overlooking a green sward, Jerard saw the bodies of four men swinging in the freshening breeze. The gibbets were still unweathered, and at the base of one there were shavings of wood that showed the haste and newness of their erection for the execution of delinquent citizens, witches and adulterers. He almost felt the grey sweat of death and hoped that Wyatt and the others would remain calm if they saw and recognized any of the corpses.

Jerard produced the official documents with great solemnity, and the officer glanced at the royal seal and the seals of the other leaders of the Royalist army. 'They send Frenchmen now to parley,' said the man with a sneer.

Jerard gave a careless laugh. 'Is it any wonder, my friend, when you have such greetings for visitors?' He gestured towards the swinging bodies and turned away. He was admitted to the spartan rooms where the Commander lived and waited while he read the papers. No tapestries on the bare walls, no rich furniture; such frugality, thought Jerard with dismay. How could any civilized man live in such surroundings? The ale that a man brought in pewter mugs was sour, and Jerard made no attempt to eat the piece of bread and cheese set on the table.

'You are not hungry?' Colonel Russell smiled coldly. 'I eat as my men eat, and we share as God meant us to share.' He eyed the Frenchman with interest. 'You have eyes that miss nothing, so take back all you see and tell the Prince how well we have repaired the Close, and how fast we are within its walls with supplies of food and armaments enough to last for six months, and the Lord Protector's armies growing in strength daily.' Jerard nodded as if agreeing. 'And tell them how we deal with traitors and delinquents who offer no submission to the cause, giving death or imprisonment to all who mock Parliament and our God-fearing ways.'

'But you battered the cathedral,' Jerard ventured. 'It is harmed.'

'It is but blocks of stone that sheltered the dissolute and the Bishop's idolaters. We have put it to better use and send our prayers to Heaven without the cant of candles and rich vestments and profligate priests.'

The tone of rigid fanaticism was chilling, and Jerard wished that he was out in the April sunshine. 'One of our horses has a stone or a thorn in his hoof,' he said. 'Have you a farrier who could look at him before we return to Sir Edwin?'

'There is one in a cottage in Quonians Lane.' Colonel Russell shrugged. 'He is a good workman, and related to one of my men, but gives no sign of joining us in war. He has set up his forge there and gives us no trouble as he is useful with our mounts. He leads a sober life so we have no quarrel with him. Go there and tell him I sent you, then return to Sir Edwin Clinton and tell him that Prince Rupert will do well to stay in Birmingham and not trouble us with his flea bites of old muskets and rusty swords.'

Jerard gathered his men and they rode to Quonians Lane without attracting much attention now that they had been admitted to the Close for words with the Commander. John Levett heard them clattering along the lane and came out of the forge wearing his leather apron. He dashed the sweat of labour from his brow, waved a greeting and returned to the anvil to finish fashioning an arm to a gate before the metal cooled.

Jerard followed him and the other men went away to deliver the letters to the imprisoned Governor, now that they had been given permission by Colonel Russell, but they went on foot to remain inconspicuous and to mingle with the citizens who were now emerging from their houses as morning strengthened.

'Lady Hester sent food and fresh butter,' Jerard said. 'There are letters from her and from your sister, and Sir Edwin would like you to come to him with your wife should there be trouble here.'

'My sister? How is she? Lucy will be sad that she couldn't

come with you today.' He smiled, and his mouth had the soft-
ness that Jerard remembered that Hope had when she was
amused. So John *was* her blood brother, but he had a heaviness
in his features that had no roots in an aristocratic sire.

'Mistress Hope is better, I think.' He saw John's sudden
alarm. 'Ah, you did not know. As soon as you left after your
wedding, on which I congratulate you with all my heart, my
friend, she was thrown from her pony and suffered many
pains. We found her and I carried her back to the house where
she recovers fast but has many bruises that take away her
loveliness for a while.' He took a bridle from a hook and
handled it with appreciation for the fine workmanship. 'Tell
me, my friend, is she your sister or a half-sister?' He shrugged
as if idly curious. 'The servants at the manor say that you had
different fathers.'

John plunged the hot metal into a bath of water and when
the seething stopped, looked up. 'It is true,' he said plainly. 'I
wish it were not so, but she was born in wedlock and so there
is no finger of scorn pointed at her.' He reached for a rasp to
trim the horn on one of the horse's hooves and to remove the
stone that Jerard had sworn must be there as an excuse to see
John Levett, but it was never found.

'Why do you wish that if it gives her grace and beauty and
great intelligence?'

'No man here would make her his wife precisely because
she has those attributes. Yeomen and farmers want sturdy
wives who can milk and toss hay and say nowt, and I want
better than for her to be the mistress of some fine runt of a
high-born litter.' John wiped his face with a cloth and passed
a hand over the shining coat of the stallion. 'She is safe with

91

Lady Hester, but may get ideas above what she can expect from life.' His level gaze was hard. 'I will kill any man who tries to take her against her will.'

'And I would help you, my friend,' said Jerard simply. He put the bridle back on its hook and wiped the grease from his hands. 'I saw much damage to the stonework of the cathedral, and heaps of glass from the coloured windows.'

John sighed. 'I hate what they have done there. They rant about religion but defile God's house and mock the teaching of the Church. They allow no marriages there, but have sham ceremonies that take the Church teachings lightly. They took a calf and dressed it richly and then baptized it as a Christian child would be baptized, in the sacred font that has been revered for generations. They baptized the cloven hoof! They hang people for witchcraft and consorting with the Devil, and yet they worship his ways,' John said bitterly.

'In such times, it is the wicked who do this and it may not be on the orders of the leaders. It is a time for weak men to crawl out from under stones and take revenge for any petty slights they may have suffered at the hands of stronger men,' Jerard averred solemnly. 'Your Lucy and her mother might have suffered greatly if you had not protected them.' He laughed. 'When the King returns, they will crawl away and hide, and others will do the same bad acts in the name of the Crown!'

'You must go back. I shall make the shutters fast and put Lucy in the cellar if an army comes.' John picked up the letter from Sir Edwin that stated that he was a part of his household and was not in Cromwell's army. It also gave him credit for fine workmanship and skill with horses, which Sir Edwin knew would have more weight as a reference than any vow of allegiance, as good farriers were hard to find in wartime. 'You must thank him for this, and if I am killed, I know that they will look after my wife and my sister,' John added.

'I, too, will see that they come to no harm,' said Jerard, and the two men clasped hands and parted with some emotion.

Jerard gave a sharp whistle to gather his men. They mounted and trotted, out of the city and along the road to the manor. Once clear, they stopped for ale and bread in a small inn, and Jerard sent two men to stay by the Birmingham Road to watch for the Royalist army and to bring word of any of Colonel Russell's men in ambush.

'You return with only four men?' Sir Edwin ran out of the house and caught the stallion's bridle. 'We grew anxious when you didn't come back by noon.'

Jerard dismounted and smiled. 'I left two to watch the Birmingham Road and to bring us word of any ambush that Colonel Russell might lay there. One will come here as soon as they see the first of the vanguard.'

'You said nothing to the Colonel of the march?'

Jerard shook his head. 'I did not like what I saw in the city, sir. They do not smile and they eat food fit only for the dungheap. No man can enjoy living if he is not fed, and I was offered no wine but some thin, brackish ale that would curdle the stomach!'

'You shall do better here,' said Sir Edwin. He called for men to take the horses. 'We shall all eat together, then you shall tell me all you saw and heard in Lichfield.'

The men sat round a table in a small salon and fell upon roasted hare and broiled fish with a hunger that made talk impossible for ten minutes. Then, gradually, Edwin learned that the old governor was well, but thin and plotting to escape from the gaol; the families that had lived in the neighbouring farms were also safe, with the exception of one who had called on God for vengeance to strike Cromwell and all his stable; and it was rumoured that many who worked on the land would be released to raise crops for the army, if they would now swear a vow of allegiance to Parliament.

'One way or another, they force allegiance, and many now accept that the Roundheads will win and make the King pass laws to fit the new way of government.' Wyatt frowned. 'I hate their way of thinking, but no man will be safe until this quarrel is over. I shall fight for the King if need be, because I believe in the Church, but when it is over, I shall have to keep quiet whoever is in power and pick up the pieces.'

Jerard glanced at the man's red hair and grinned. '*Très difficile* for you, my friend. Today, I thought to lose you twice when your face flamed, but you held your tongue and all was well.'

Edwin stood up as a sign that the men might leave for their own quarters. 'Make the stables fast and put as many horses as you can in the barns with a guard on the door. Royalist or Roundhead, they all want nags and we have no need to supply them. Put this paper on the oak tree by the lodge. It bears the Prince's seal and gives us immunity to his troops. There are empty farms enough for billeting his men and we have done our duty, risking life and property to bring messages to both sides.'

'And if the Prince wishes to visit Lady Hester?'

'He will be as welcome as any Christian gentleman,' Edwin replied gravely. 'They are old friends.'

94

'Are the ladies well?' asked Jerard politely.

Edwin regarded him with a glance that made the young man shift his gaze. 'Well indeed, sir. My wife is recovering from my long absence with much joy, and her ward, Mistress Hope, has lost her aches and pains and sits in a chair by the window.'

'Your ward, sir?'

'She is as our own now. Not of our blood, but very close to our hearts and we know of her family and antecedents, so in these troubled times, it is well that we own her as our ward, protect her and make her ready for a suitable marriage. She is sixteen and we shall give her a small dowry.'

'In France, such marriages are arranged with no joy,' said Jerard, strangely upset by what he had heard.

'In England, too,' Edwin admitted. 'Many royal alliances have been made with no thought for the couple who have to bed together and make heirs. Many great houses join forces and fortunes to make them even more powerful, just by linking one unwilling child to another.'

'I heard that she has a father who may have legal power over her,' said Jerard. 'He has vowed that Francis Turner, a base fellow in the army, may have her.' His face was pale and he recalled John Levett's expression when he swore that Francis should never lay a finger on his sister.

'You are concerned, my boy? You met her only briefly and can have no idea of her nature. You may not buss her as you might a maid, and your family would never allow a solemn union.'

Jerard moved restlessly. 'In France these things are possible. We do not condemn mistakes in the bedchamber, or look so closely if the blood is right, and I am not the heir to the title.'

'Hope is in our care and we shall protect her from Francis Turner, whatever is said. She is as a daughter to my wife, and I love my wife,' he added firmly.

'You cannot come out openly against such a man!' Jerard leaned on the table to give his words emphasis. 'It would be putting yourself and all you hold dear into the power of the army. I saw the barren fields of those who spoke against the regime, and there must be many who eye you with suspicion and envy.' He stood back, tall and dignified. 'I, myself, Sir Edwin, will take on this task. I have nothing to lose here but my life and the honour of this lady. I shall fight for her if it is needed, and I offer my sword for her now.'

'You will then put yourself on the side of the King? There is no other way. Who chooses to fight Francis Turner and Levett is their enemy, and the enemy of Cromwell. Take care, my boy, and consider before you make any decision.'

'May I see the ladies?' The old, bold humour was back. 'How can I decide if I am deprived of her company?'

'You must swear not to tell her of what we have spoken. You must give your word that you will treat her with all respect and do nothing with haste.'

'I swear to treat her with respect, sir,' was all he said, and when Hope looked up and saw him in the doorway, once more washed and fresh and as brightly dressed as a tropical bird of paradise, she felt her heart leap in her breast and her eyes showed that she had thought of him and was now happy.

'I am glad to see you well, madam,' he said. He took one bandaged hand in both of his and kissed the wrist. 'You tremble, but you do not draw away as once you did. You are not frightened of me, little bird?'

'A little,' whispered Hope.

'There, I sit beside you and hold your hand so. It does not hurt and we can talk about – what?'

'Tell me about France,' Hope said, with shining eyes. 'Is it true that they eat frogs and snails, and the women in Court wear wigs as high as a yard and have dresses dampened to cling to their bodies?'

'They are no different from the ladies of the English Court. Although in these hard times, the French are the first in fashion and the ladies of the Court here have to wait for many new dresses.'

'Lady Hester says that you must go back soon,' Hope said at last. Her eyes lost their sparkle.

'And you are promised to a man chosen by your father, Sam Levett,' he said gravely, and a pulse in his neck beat deeply and fast.

'No! I am with Lady Hester now. They cannot touch me, can they?' The fear in her eyes made him want to take her into a passionate embrace, but he forced his voice to remain calm and merely put an arm round her shoulders.

'You do not like the idea? Marriage to a man in favour with Cromwell?'

'I would rather be burned as a witch,' she said in a low voice.

'There are other fates,' he said mildly. 'Other men.'

Hope blushed and tears shone unshed on her eyelashes. 'I am not like my mother,' she whispered. 'I shall die an old maid.'

He threw back his head and laughed. 'An old maid? Is that what you say here? We are more polite and say the virgin lady of whatever age is *comme une jeune fille*, like a young girl.'

Hope smiled. 'You will stay here for a few more days?'

He bent and kissed one of the bruises on her brow. ' I must stay to see what you are like without so many colours on your face. That is not a fashion I wish to see in France, and you would need more than patches to hide all those bruises, but when you are well, we shall ride together.'

# VII

Even the birds seemed to wait in silence. Dawn came with a mist on the distant hills and a chill on the breath that made small clouds as the horses stood in the spinney. Stacks of willow wands tied up in bunches lay abandoned by the basket makers, who had cut them before they had heard of armies coming their way, and the men waiting blew on fingers as cold as they had been in winter.

Horses approached from the north and the waiting men saw that the horsemen were from the manor come to relieve their watch. 'We thought you had been taken by the Devil,' said Wyatt. 'Why leave the farm and come out here? Have you been here all night?'

'We heard sounds and couldn't see the crossroads, so we came back to warn the Prince of possible ambush from Watling Street, but it was only cattle that wander unfenced and have no masters.'

'Sir Edwin had word that the Prince camped across Bourne Brook and will come this morning,' Wyatt told them. 'Go back and tell them that all is well here, and we shall stay in the farm and wait.'

'Do you ride with the Prince?' asked one of the men. 'I shall be glad to be out of it. I am no soldier, and the sooner I can get back to tailoring the more use I shall be.'

'The Prince might need you,' said Wyatt, grinning. 'He'll need a new silk shirt after camping and braving the mud of the Bourne.'

'Then he can give me back my shop in Lichfield, and let me get on with my work,' he replied sourly. 'What profit is there when the Roundheads wear only strong dark fustian and have no thought for fashion? Their clothes last forever and do us all out of our living.'

Wyatt and his companion rode with them to the crossroads, where the old road to York crossed the Roman road to Shrewsbury, and went into the shelter of a deserted barn by the farm gate. A small fire under a black pot burned fitfully and warmed a jug of ale. The night guard drank and left, and as morning advanced, Wyatt began to wonder if the Prince had lost his courage as no man or beast passed the farm.

Suddenly, a black line of crows beat a way from the trees lining the road and made a noisy retreat to the shelter of the woods, and other birds took up the alarm call. Four armed men rode slowly along the road and paused by the farm as if looking for trouble, but found instead a paper pinned to the wood that told them they would meet no resistance.

There was a shout, and more men rode to join the first ones. Wyatt emerged slowly with a white handkerchief tied to a stick. 'I have a message from Sir Edwin Clinton,' he shouted, and the men ordered him to advance and be seen.

The officer read the note and handed it to his sergeant to take back to the Prince. 'Is this true?' he asked Wyatt.

'It says the way is clear to Lichfield but the Roundheads are walled up within the Close and invulnerable.' He laughed and boasted. 'Their spies have not told them of the strength of this army. We shall have them out before tomorrow night.' He looked with hard eyes at the two men. 'Do you come from the City?'

'I did,' said Wyatt, 'but am now with Sir Edwin and serve him at the manor.'

'And do you serve the King?'

'I serve my master,' said Wyatt. He grinned. 'I know Lichfield and have no patience with men who never laugh. I have a map to show you side alleys and tunnels under the city, with marks to show where all who are faithful to the King are imprisoned. Release them and you will have all the help you need to position your guns. I have written the names of good bakers, and a butcher who hangs venison well and there is a farrier in Quonians Lane who looks neither to left nor right but does his work with horses from any stable. You will have no treachery from him but beware of his father, the man in the second cottage, who by now might have changed his coat. His name is Sam Levett and his crony, Francis Turner, is known as a spy. They might shelter under the strength of the farrier John Levett. His sister is connected with the Clintons at the manor.'

'And the citizens of Lichfield, are they for the King?'

'They will be for anyone who treats them with justice and makes life easier for them. They will let you enter the town and watch, as we all must,' he added frankly. His face darkened. 'Parliament men have desecrated the cathedral and hanged many good men and women in their witch hunts and because of pointing fingers that denounce innocent men to settle private quarrels. That makes the people favour the Crown. It is the centre of life there, and sacred to the memory of all our forebears.'

Wyatt and his man rode with the army for four miles and then went to report, back to Sir Edwin.

'They rest tonight in a farm about two miles from the City and will ride in at dawn,' he told Sir Edwin. 'They look in fine fettle and the horses are not weary. Perhaps the tide will turn if they take the City.'

'I am afraid for the Crown,' said Edwin. 'Parliament is firm in London and has the buildings of Whitehall and Parliament in its hands so that people who look to the centre of government for guidance will come to accept the rule of Cromwell, and the King will lose much of his power even after the peace is made.' He sighed. 'There are even men who shout for the head of our sovereign but we as a nation are not murderers of kings.'

Jerard Barill listened while he polished the fine crossbow with an oiled square of cloth. 'Do we hunt today, Sir Edwin?' he asked. 'Your horses need to be kept fit and your men to have a keen eye.'

'No, we keep quiet and let no man say we take sides in this dispute,' Edwin said firmly. 'Hunting with crossbows and duck guns might give spies the wrong idea of our intentions, and there have been men lurking in the woods ready to make much of a little. My keepers took one for a poacher and filled him with buckshot and he left in a hurry, walking his horse, but we can't swear that every man in the woods is poaching.'

'Then I must entertain the ladies,' said Jerard. He put the crossbow into its leather case and hung it with his saddle.

Edwin watched as he strode into the house and wondered if he was sincere. His eyes showed the healthy lust of a young man for a pretty girl and his glance was soft whenever Hope appeared, at the table now or in the salon with Lady Hester. He made them laugh and played music for them and was teaching Hope to sing a small poem in French, amazed at the quickness of her ear and her enthusiasm for the music.

'You will play for us?' asked Lady Hester. 'But first I must see my husband and hear the news from Wyatt. Call for sack and almond biscuits, my dear, and I shall be with you both shortly.'

Jerard stood by Hope's side as she threaded fine blue ribbons into a petticoat and tied the narrow silk into soft bows. 'You work hard,' he said, amused at her concentration.

'I have so much to repay,' she said sincerely. 'Lady Hester treats me as if I were her own daughter and I want to serve her as best I can.'

'You will leave her one day,' he said, watching her face. 'What if a man asks you to go away far from the Clintons?'

'That is unlikely, sir.' She sewed a ragged end and made it neat, then bit the sewing silk with sharp white teeth and refused to look at him directly. 'My place is here and I have no suitors but the man to whom my father said I must be wed.'

'If another should ask for you and you found him to your liking, what then?'

Her eyes filled with tears. 'It is wicked to tease me, sir,' she said, and bent over her work, which she could no longer see. The memory of her own mother haunted her. She recalled the sad eyes and the many tears and the thin body deprived of love and food. Hope had noticed more as she grew older and sensed the atmosphere in the cottage, with the unhappy woman tied to Sam Levett while Hope was small and there was no escape. She had not been strong enough to return to Lady Hester's service, and had died young.

So, men took the maidenhead and tossed the flower away. Hope stitched the lace on a cap and made her finger bleed; it was still painful when she tried to hold a fine needle. Most of the bruising had subsided and her natural bloom emerged under the dark lashes. Jerard took away the cap and the needle and kissed her fingers where the nails had been torn. He turned her hand over and smiled at the remaining red stain from the herbs that Jane Willow had used.

'You are healed,' he said. 'You are very beautiful, *ma chère*.'

'My hands look dirty, but I scrubbed them and put on unguent that Jane Willow made so they may be better soon,' she said, but had no strength to take her hand away.

'Not dirty,' he said. 'In a country across the seas where they have elephants and strange dress, the women paint their palms red as a sign of beauty.'

She looked up in disbelief, but he was not laughing. 'You have seen these things, sir?'

'No, but now I can believe it to be true. I find your hands *ravissant*, even with the broken nails.'

She tried to draw away but he brought her closer, his face on her hair, and she held her breath while he kissed her brow and eyelids and then held her away from him.

'I must not,' he said. 'I promised Sir Edwin that I would take no liberty with you, madam, but I think you like me a little.'

She nodded dumbly. Was this how it began? Was this the feeling that had made her mother lose her mind and go with a man who said he loved her? A man such as this, sophisticated and sure of himself, with wealth and position and no idea of the suffering he could cause?

He laughed. 'I am bad and yet I teach you French, which is good. Say after me, *Je t'aime, Jerard.*'

'What does it mean?' Hope blushed, seeing his laughing eyes. 'You mock me, sir.'

He took her hands again gently and looked into her face. 'No. They are words I wish to hear from your lips, madam. I want to hear them in my own tongue.'

'What does it mean? I must say them in English first and know the meaning.'

'Later . . .' he murmured, as Lady Hester came into the room. 'I see that the poor hands heal fast, Lady Hester,' he said, with a wicked glance at her troubled face when she saw him holding the hands of her ward. 'Now I will play for you, and Mistress Hope shall sing the words I taught her.'

'Is it a song?' Hope's expression cleared. 'Mr Barill taught me some more words, Lady Hester. Play the music for them and I will try to say it as you did.'

'Not those words. Sing what I taught you yesterday,' he said hastily.

Lady Hester gave him a cool and knowing look and settled herself in her chair as if she would never budge again, picked up her tapestry and silks and listened with a slightly sad smile as the two young people sang and laughed together. She saw that Hope was fascinated by the handsome Frenchman.

If Charles were here I would be happy indeed, she thought. He would protect Hope and yet allow her to have the freedom of the house and the company of any visitors. Then she recalled her feelings when she had thought that even Charles might become enamoured of the pretty girl who had filled the empty corners of her life at the manor.

'*Non*! You say it so . . . ' said Jerard. 'You remember well, but you have no . . . *français*. You must say it so.' He repeated the words with an exaggerated accent to amuse her and Hope laughed and managed a good imitation.

'I asked Mr West to come here,' said Lady Hester. 'When I heard that he had been taken from his parish and forbidden to give the sacraments, I obtained a place for him to teach mathematics and languages in the schools in Lichfield. He may do so even under the eye of the Roundheads if he does not teach religious studies, but first he needs care as he has been ill, and if he stays with us then we may have the comfort of his ministry in secret. I have told the servants that I want him to teach Hope many subjects that will ease her position when I take her with me to meet important people, so he may remain here if he wishes and be safe, as even Lord Cromwell appreciates the learning of such men and schooling from priests is sought by many among his own officers.'

Hope looked apprehensive. 'I am not fit for such teaching, Lady Hester.'

'It will fill your time when you are not with me,' she said, with a meaningful glance at Jerard. 'I should be happier to know that you are occupied with books while I am away from you, and I shall listen at times and learn also as my education was sadly neglected in French and Latin.'

Jerard put away his music and bowed. 'I must see that my horse is better,' he said formally. He smiled at Hope. 'You need have no fear, little one. Lady Hester is like a guard who watches you and keeps you from harm.' He stepped closer so that Lady Hester couldn't hear. 'You may learn much French, which is good, but you will not enjoy it as much as my teaching. *Au revoir. Je t'aime*, Mistress Hope.'

Hope laughed. So the phrase was an amusement and no more, spoken so lightheartedly. *'Je t'aime, Jerard,'* she said, and blushed as she saw his eyes brighten with tenderness. Abruptly, he walked away and left them to their sewing.

'What was he saying?' asked Hester.

'He taught me words, but wouldn't say what they mean.' Hope frowned. 'They are not wicked or lewd, I trust. He would not teach me such things. I know the meaning of the song and other phrases, but not that one.'

'Tell me,' said Hester.

Hope lifted her glance from the embroidery and her innocence made Hester want to hug her close and keep her safe from all predators. 'He made me say, *Je t'aime, Jerard*, when he said, *Je t'aime*, Mistress Hope.'

'He trifles with you, Hope! He makes you use the familiar French that is kept for family and those we love, and not said between strangers.'

'But he is not a stranger,' Hope protested. 'I like him and he likes me and he is amusing.'

'You like him; yes, my dear, but in French he made you say, "I love you, Jerard".'

'And he said, "I love you, Mistress Hope".' Her lips parted and trembled.

'He teases you as all men tease pretty women,' snapped Hester crossly. 'He is too bold and I wish he might keep away from you.' She prayed that the priest would come soon and fill the girl's head with something other than fruitless dreams, and when Mr West arrived just before dinner was brought in, late because the men had been busy working the horses, Lady Hester bent her head when they gathered to eat, delighted that a priest might say grace at her table, and prayed for the return of the stability and safety of the Church.

The words, spoken in Latin, were balm and reassurance to her, but Hope could think only of the tiny phrase in French that had made her admit her love for Jerard Barill. She glanced across at him where he now tore bread apart and dipped it in the soup before eating it daintily. He was laughing and listening to the tale that Sir Edwin was telling the men, laughing as if he had never looked serious and tender and had never said, 'I love you, Mistress Hope'.

To her consternation, Hope was sent to the big study that was lined with so many books that she wondered if they had all been opened, leave alone read, and she was made to feel as if she were at school. The priest gave her a passage to read and when he saw that she was literate and intelligent, began to teach her simple mathematics. The huge wall clock struck four and then five, and Dorcas came to find her because Lady Hester wanted to have her hair dressed.

'Tomorrow, we will learn French and Latin,' Mr West said.

'Lady Hester does not want you to be tired,' said Hope, in an attempt to have some free time from lessons.

'Lady Hester is a blessed soul and I shall serve her well,' he insisted. 'I shall teach you to the glory of God as I can no longer observe the Mass, and as you learn fast, I shall be proud of my pupil.'

'You are kind, sir,' said Hope miserably. She tried to forget that Jerard had asked her to ride with him the next morning and she had not seen him since dinner.

'You must not try your eyes too much with books,' Lady Hester said as Hope went into her boudoir. 'I need you now, and Mr West must refresh himself before supper.'

'He is tired,' said Hope. 'He talks of so many lessons that I fear he will be exhausted.'

'I shall speak to him,' said Hester. 'Two hours each morning and again later in the day will suffice, as I need you and you must have time to see to your own clothes. What lessons tomorrow?' Hope was brushing her hair for her, and lightly glossed with jasmine oil the pale blonde tresses that were now touched with silver but still beautiful.

'Latin and French in the morning,' said Hope.

'You will learn more than the empty phrases taught by that jackanapes,' Hester said sternly. 'He asked if you could ride with him tomorrow, but my husband does not think it safe as there are strangers in the woods and they may be spies or highwaymen lurking in wait for people fleeing the armies.'

'Is there news from Lichfield, Lady Hester?' Hope was almost relieved to be forbidden to be alone with Jerard as her emotions were in a turmoil. I have not met men like him, she told herself, so how can I know his true heart?

'The Prince entered without a shot being fired,' replied Lady Hester.

'They have taken Lichfield for the King?' Hope's eyes shone.

'They have taken the town, but the Close is sealed fast with many defences and guns and the Parliamentarians refuse to parley. How can anyone broach those walls or get across the

moat and through the portcullis and doors since they strengthened every weak point in the defences? There are many
citizens inside the Close held hostage to good terms and they
say that with food for six months the Royalists will tire first if
the weather worsens.'

'I wonder about my brother,' said Hope. The tone of her
voice made Hester turn sharply. Hope was very pale. 'And
Lucy is there and might be in danger if the soldiers learn that
she is married to a Levett.'

'A Levett who is not like his father,' asserted Hester, and
wished she could convince herself that all those honest
people she knew in Lichfield would emerge safe from the
coming conflict. 'Jane Willow will be safe now, Mr West will
be able to say Mass and I can wear emeralds and furs in
public again if the Prince drives out the Roundheads. They
have opened up the gaols and released the Governor's men
and are rounding up spies and those who openly served the
Colonel, so I suppose the gaols will be as full again before
nightfall.'

Hope twisted the fair hair in a band of pearls and pinned
the matching brooch to the décolletage of the ice-blue taffeta
dress. Hester sighed with pleasure. 'You make me look young
again, Hope. Go now and dress. Wear the velvet dress that you
and Dorcas made.'

'But that is for very grand occasions, madam.' Hope caught
her breath as she had been permitted only to fit on the dress
when it was finished, and then had seen it hung in the closet
to await the dim and very distant celebration of Hester's birth-
day or next Christmas.

'What better occasion?' said Hester with a smile. 'His

Majesty will take Lichfield and all England will see that he must come back to full power.'

'Is it wise to celebrate a Royalist victory, Lady Hester?' Hope was torn between the desire to wear the lovely gown and her instinct for prudence, knowing that Sir Edwin had to be scrupulous in his neutrality. She recalled his anger when a groom insulted a soldier who had called at the house to get water for his horse and perhaps a bite to eat in the kitchen, and her early life had made her cautious of what was said among the servants.

'Then we must think of another reason for celebration. The safe return of Sir Edwin is sufficient and I shall say nothing to offend any spies listening,' Hester said ruefully. 'You are right, Hope. I must be careful, especially as we keep a priest within our walls.'

'Then I may wear the dress?'

Hester laughed at the sudden incredulous joy in the girl's eyes. 'Yes, you may wear the dress and the shoes and take these trinkets to hide the bruises on your throat and arms. Wear a light shawl, and with some more of the lotion that Jane Willow prepared, you will be pretty again.' She regarded Hope with a mixture of approval and doubt. 'Yes, you must wear fine clothes now, and be used to them when we go forth to the soirées that must now be allowed. I can't have a draggletail girl with me who is afraid to soil her hem as she walks. Ladies must go about as if they have an army of servants to clear up after them and pay no heed to the work they cause.' She laughed. 'We take care when at home, but in company, it is important to be more careless and to impress people with our wealth and power, or what noble family would want to marry my Charles to one of their daughters?'

'You would arrange such a marriage?'

'If Charles could marry and love where money is, then that would please me most,' said Hester. 'I was fortunate that the man chosen for me was Sir Edwin, whom I had loved since a child and who loved me.' She glanced at Hope, curiously watching her reaction. 'I hear that Jerard Barill has been told of the girl he should marry in France, but he seems in no hurry to rush to the altar.'

Hope froze, and one of the dainty necklaces that Hester had so generously given her slipped from her fingers. She bent to pick it up and gulped to regain her composure. Never again must I let him touch me and hold my hand. Never must I allow those gentle, disturbing kisses on my face and hands, she vowed, with an empty heart. 'This necklace and this bracelet and choker will suit the dress well, madam,' she said, and hurried from the room, leaving the rest of the jewellery on the table.

Dorcas, who had now become accustomed to Hope's new position and was amused more than resentful by her elevation in the household, came to help her dress. Hope was no longer a threat to the pecking order in the servants' quarters, and she relieved Dorcas of the need to travel in jolting coaches and to meet people she didn't trust or like. She helped her to slip into the tightly fitting, deep blue velvet gown and brushed the tawny swathes of hair to fit into a chaplet of silver. Hope smoothed on the cream that Jane had made and it smelled of violets. Her hands were almost smooth again and the nails were growing.

'You look as pretty as a picture, Miss Hope,' said Dorcas with the pride of one who had helped to make the gown. She pulled the neckline lower and tied the velvet and silver choker round the slender throat, and when the other jewellery adorned the white skin, Hope gasped at her reflection in the yellowish glass on the wall of her room. In spite of her sadness when she thought of Jerard, promised in France to some unknown woman, her natural liveliness and humour surfaced. 'I wish I had a fan like the ladies of the Court,' she said, her eyes sparkling. 'They say that messages are passed between the ladies and the courtiers by means of gestures made by the fans.'

'Happen you'd make the wrong one, not knowing, and then you'd be in a fine pickle!' laughed Dorcas. 'A girl with pretty eyes can do more than an old fan, but be careful where you look as some of those in at supper tonight would have you in the hay as soon as kiss your hand.'

'I shall look down and be very demure, Dorcas,' Hope promised, but Dorcas clucked under her breath as Hope ran across to the boudoir to see if Lady Hester had everything she needed before supper.

'You watch your step, my girl,' she muttered. 'Your mother came to bed by Lord Victor Dusquesne by all accounts, and bastardy makes no dowry.'

To add to Hester's joy, there were letters from her son and news of people he had met on his travels. Hope found her reading them. When Jerard Barill came to the boudoir asking if he might take the ladies to supper, he was with Hester before Hope appeared.

'Madame, I know that man and the ones he mentions. They are good friends of mine and came with other English gentlemen when I met Charles in Lyons,' he was saying before he saw Hope. 'Charles gave them his address and an open invitation to visit you when they are in England. They make great sport, and even the older man is quite a buck, with a keen eye for game and as keen an eye for a pretty girl.'

Hope stood in the doorway and listened. Hester looked flustered. 'They are coming here?' she asked, as if they would not be welcome.

'Lord Dusquesne was enchanted when he heard that Charles lived here. He said that he knew your house, Madame, many years ago, and had spent a few very happy weeks here. It will be good to mend old acquaintance, *n'est-ce pas*?'

'He may not come,' said Hester, as if to convince herself. 'The time is not right for visitors to be free to move over the land. It could be dangerous.'

'Am I in danger? I think that I am safer than your own family, Madame, as I carry letters of credence and have no loyalty to either warring faction. If they visit you I may stay and go back to France with them for company.'

He saw Hope and stood up slowly, then advanced and took her hand to kiss. His words were soft and Hope understood nothing that he said, but his hand transferred his latent passion into her own small palm. He was pale and his eyes held a glint that Hope dared not meet. She stood passively until he let her hand rest against the velvet dress once more.

'Who are these new guests?' Hope asked, to break the silence.

'They are not welcome in my house,' said Hester, with vehemence. 'I shall ask Edwin to say that we cannot, in these hard times, entertain any visitors.'

'You have taken me into your home with warmth and

generosity, and you have many guests, Madame!' Jerard looked confused. 'I have met them and they are friends of Charles now. Is it right to refuse his friends who have given him hospitality and want nothing but to meet you again?' He struck his chest. 'They are as I am, French and of high birth, mannerly and I hope amusing.'

'I like to believe that you are different,' said Hester softly. She looked at Hope and wished the girl was dressed in a loose shift of dun-coloured coarse wool and that the bruises hadn't cleared up so quickly. Hester placed a hand on Jerard's arm. 'We must go down. Hope, stay and tidy my dressing table and join us in five minutes.'

# VIII

The fat cousin from Alrewas almost blocked any view that Jerard could glimpse of Hope at the supper table and she was wedged between the cousin and a Royalist officer who said nothing but attacked his food as though he were moving his troops, slicing meat with a knife, that he had produced from its sheath, of such terrifying sharpness that Hope wondered what would happen if it slipped and he found he was eating his own thumb.

An air of tension made most people talk loudly and too fast, and Hope was able to remain quiet except when the fat cousin nudged her to hear one of his lewd jokes and expected her to laugh.

All that filled her mind was the fact that she loved Jerard and that her first resolution had been impossible to keep. How could she avoid physical contact when it was polite to shake hands, to have hands kissed, especially by foreigners, for shawls to be adjusted over shoulders and wine to be passed from hand to hand with murmured pleasantries? The fine Malmsey wine that Jerard had brought her when the guests were assembling had brought colour to her cheeks and a

117

brightness to her eyes that owed as much to the unshed tears as to the wine.

'What's he doing here?' asked the fat cousin in a hoarse whisper. 'Spies everywhere, my dear, and Cousin Edwin should know better than to have any from either camp at his table.'

'Lady Hester said that he came tonight in order to bring Sir Edwin to Lichfield tomorrow to see if a peace can be made before they begin fighting. He is Captain Nichols of the Prince's guard,' whispered Hope.

'Edwin makes a good go-between,' he said. 'Thought I'd do well in the diplomatic field myself, but I couldn't get away from my farm and I can't abide all the foreign jackanapes they have at Whitehall.'

Hope nodded, as if she knew how much the country had lost and that he would have done well in Whitehall. She listened to a long story about local politics, or she seemed to listen but her thoughts were her own and she had no idea of what she ate.

Hester glanced at the pale solemn face from time to time and ached for the girl. If Dusquesne came and put two and two together, it would take no more than a glance to recognize the Dusquesne hair and nose and to awaken old scandals. Her mother is dead and so spared such a confrontation, she thought, but there are many who recall the days when the gallant young man pursued the handsome girl with casual relentlessness and left her with child.

As if this thought had found its way into the head of the cousin, he turned to look at Hope more intently than at any time during the meal. 'You've a look about you, girl, that I can't place. Not Edwin's, are you? No, not that. It will come to me,' he said importantly. 'Never forget a face and you've the look of someone I've met.'

'My mother is dead and Lady Hester has taken me as her ward,' Hope explained, wondering how many times in the future it would be necessary to repeat this when people grew curious.

He nodded to the servant to refill his goblet and attacked his food again with as much vigour as Hope's other neighbour was eating his meat, then at last, the men were replete and the ladies moved away into the small salon to talk and leave the men to plan for tomorrow. Hope cast one almost despairing glance towards Jerard and knew that he was watching her straight, slim back as she swept out in the wake of the ladies, her hair glistening under the silver chaplet and the soft glow of the velvet gown moulding to her thighs as she walked.

Edwin waved to the men to gather at one end of the vast table and the servants cleared the dishes and brought more wine and sweetmeats. 'It grows late, and we must leave early tomorrow. The Prince is setting up guns to overlook the Cathedral Close from the mount beyond Gaia Lane and has placed men by St John's Hostel to make ready to receive the wounded. The keepers of Milley's Hospital may have more than old women to tend if the fighting grows hot. I fear for the city if the guns from the Close fire on its inhabitants to make Prince Rupert retreat, so every atttempt must be made to prevent bloodshed.'

'We are determined to attack, and to free the cathedral,' Captain Nichols stated firmly. 'This is not the time to parley, sir. Cromwell grows bold and takes many towns, and the men in places where they depend on the making of arms and anything made by craftsmen that may be used in war flock to his banner or their livelihood is gone.'

'The farmers are for the King,' said the cousin. 'We have no time for men of steel with no appetite for good food or wine or gracious living, and the sooner we send them off with their tails between their legs, the sooner this country will return to sanity and peace.' The priest nodded but said nothing, being far too relieved to be out of Lichfield and under the protection of Sir Edwin to give any opinion. He sipped his wine and thought of the lessons he had not quite finished preparing for Hope the next day. Tutoring was satisfying when his pupils were as eager to learn and intelligent as Lady Hester's ward.

Chairs scraped back over the polished wooden floor and the men either drifted away to their quarters or joined the ladies for music, and after a short interval of entertainment, when Jerard played and two of the ladies sang, Edwin ordered his cousin's carriage and firmly stated that his household must rest. 'I shall sleep alone, my dear,' he said to Hester. 'I shall have but little sleep and may disturb you.'

'Then I shall bring Hope in by my bed,' said Hester. 'She may make a tisane before I go to sleep and be there to dress me in the morning.' She ordered the truckle bed to be made up and Miss Hope's clothes for the next day to be placed in the boudoir, and long after the girl lay like a tired kitten, fast asleep and relaxed on the hard cot, Hester lay awake and heard soft footsteps along the passageway from the gallery, and the almost soundless opening of a door. She smiled wryly.

It was to be expected: the evening had been full of good food and wine and music and a young man with thoughts of a day of possible danger and excitement would want to take the comfort of soft arms and a willing body as men everywhere did before battle.

Jerard cursed softly. The moon shone through the shutters and a silver glint showed him that the bed was unoccupied. His loins were taut and his mind fuddled by too much wine, but the empty virginal bed made him sober. He touched the pillow where Hope's hair should have hidden the white linen and smelled the rose scent from the unguent she used for her hands. He backed away as if the bed accused him and then impulsively unpinned one golden brooch from his tunic and placed it on the pillow. He went to the small desk by the window and pushed back one shutter. The moon shone as bright as day and he scribbled a note.

The ink from the brass well was thick and spluttered from the pen as he wrote too hastily. English was too cold for his emotions and yet he knew that Hope would not understand written French, so laboriously his mind translated his thoughts and at last he was satisfied.

He pinned the note to the pillow with the brooch and left the room as softly as he had entered, blowing a kiss in the direction of the firmly shut door leading to Lady Hester's bedroom. Already horses were being groomed and saddled and made ready for the party, bright and regal with silver bridles and shining saddlery of tooled leather. Jerard changed into thick breeches and boots and a fine woollen tunic with slashed sleeves and used his second brooch to pin a heavy crimson velvet cloak across his shoulders. His dull

gold velvet hat completed a picture from a renaissance paint-
ing and when Lady Hester crept to her window to watch the
men depart, but remained unseen by the party below, her
heart ached for Hope and wondered how any girl could
resist such a man.

The smell of fresh dung and animal warmth came up
through the chill morning. Lady Hester closed the shutters
and lay half-asleep for an hour before Hope stirred and woke,
too late to watch the men leave.

Captain Nichols rode ahead with Wyatt and three of his
own men, and another four came up behind the rest of the
procession of horsemen. Jerard Barill flaunted the pennant of
France and his own coat of arms and sat proudly on the black
stallion by Sir Edwin's side, a party to the diplomatic mission
on which they were bent. A thrush joined the dawn chorus,
and dew on the hedgerows polished the fresh leaves and hung
diamonds on the blossom of a rogue pear tree, planted by a
passing bird and now blending with the wild plants and
brushing off the shabby remnants of last year's traveller's joy.

Cottage windows were shuttered but there was a feeling of
eyes watching as the party rode into Lichfield. Guards at St
John's, outside the city wall, the hostel used to give shelter to
travellers arriving after the city gates were shut for the night
but now used as a guard house for troops, gave way when
they saw Captain Nichols, and the gates were swung open to
admit the heralds of neutrality. A distant church bell sounded.
It was cracked and gave tongue to the injury it had suffered in
the last bombardment, and the streets were deserted.

Jerard looked about him as Sir Edwin approached the Close,

and the Town Crier, roused from his bed as he had the loudest voice in the county, shouted greetings and the need for truce to the incumbents of the Close, but the words were met with oaths and a sermon on the wickedness and self-indulgence of the Court, and defiance was hurled into the teeth of moderation.

'They have food and water and arms, and have confidence in their defences,' said Captain Nichols. 'You have heard what they say, sir?' Sir Edwin nodded gravely. 'Then our commanders will attack and drive them out like rabbits from a burrow.'

'You would breach the walls and injure the fabric of the Holy Church?' asked Edwin. 'Your army will do as much, or more, damage as was done by Parliament men.'

'I am a simple soldier, sir. A professional Cavalier who obeys orders and fights for my Sovereign. If I have to destroy a house or a church, I obey and lose no sleep over it. We have taken prisoners who will tell us the weak points in the defences, and I believe there are secret tunnels between the great pond and the Close.' He dismounted and handed the reins to a groom. 'I must report to the Prince who is now installed in the house once occupied by the Roundhead commander.'

'*Plus ça change . . .*' murmured Jerard. 'One army goes and another comes and the city is no better, no worse but may die because of them both.'

'I shall return to the manor and await news,' said Edwin. 'If either side needs me, a fast horse can bring me word within an hour or two. I pray that a solution may be found that spills no more blood.'

'I will stay,' Jerard averred. He laughed. 'I am not a target even if I look like neither side, and with your leave, Sir Edwin, I may ride faster on this fine horse. I shall stay with John Levett in Quonians Lane and serve you there.' He sensed the older man's anxiety. 'Have no fears for me, *mon brave*. I am immortal.' His teeth flashed white and his eyes were full of the arrogance of inviolate youth.

'It would suit me well,' admitted Sir Edwin slowly, 'but you are my guest, the friend of my absent son, and you have no quarrel here.'

'It makes me a good ambassador, *nest-ce pas*? I can sport in the field behind Quonians Lane and teach Levett the art of the crossbow, and he may teach me the use of that strange rope he carries on his saddle.'

The Royalists clattered away to stable the horses and to take the first draught of the day with bread and cheese. Sir Edwin embraced the Frenchman with emotion. 'Take care, my son,' he said. 'You are like my own, and Lady Hester would never forgive me if harm befell you on my account.'

'And Mistress Hope? Would she weep for me?' His smile was cynical. 'Would *anyone* weep for us? I saw no faces watching us leave and heard no pleas urging me to stay,' he added, remembering the closed shutters when the men departed.

'My wife pleasured me last evening before we ate,' said Sir Edwin with a satisfied air. 'We agreed that I would slip away early with no wifely tears and no strain on my resolution to come on this mission.'

'I am glad for you, sir.' Sir Edwin smiled as he saw the wry grin. 'I was celibate and it pleased me not.'

'There are maids and girls from the village . . .' began Edwin.

'I want no soiled petticoats!'

'Then you must marry, or burn and die, Jerard,' he suggested gently. 'It is bad for a man to restrain his lust, and yet once married to a loving wife, all strumpets lose their attraction.' He eyed him keenly. 'It is well that you are not too much with our ward. We must look for a husband for her, and she will need her maidenhead for a dowry with the small allotment we can afford her.'

Jerard felt his colour rising. Last night he could have ruined the girl who was seldom absent from his thoughts, and he longed to go to her and have her soft lips trembling for his touch. *'Merde!'* he whispered, as he rode away towards Quonians Lane. 'You are bewitched, Jerard.'

He found John Levett by following the sound of a hammer on metal and John came from the forge as soon as he heard the hooves. Two brightly caparisoned horses stood munching hay while they waited their turn to be shod, and another stood patiently with one shoe still to be fitted.

'I heard that an envoy was coming,' said John. He shouted to Lucy to bring ale and bread and Jerard followed him in to the forge to watch him finish his work. The smell of hot metal and dry wood burning, mingled with the acrid smoke from the scorched hoof horn, made Jerard think of his own home and the stable of fine horses he had left when he came to England in search of adventure. Would the girl chosen by his parents ever fill his life? He saw only one laughing face possible as he imagined riding his own horses again, and could fit no other face to his dreams.

John slapped the rump of the last horse, and threw off his leather apron. Lucy set food on the table in the small kitchen and poured ale from a huge pewter jug. 'How is Hope?' she asked. 'We heard that she has been made a fine lady.'

'Lady Hester has made her a ward and it is fitting. She is very beautiful,' said Jerard. He watched the couple in whose cottage he now ate and observed their complete happiness in each other. The vast estates in France would be empty if he returned alone, but how could he abduct the ward of a friend and carry her off to be his mistress? He knew that any such action would alienate himself from the family that he had come to love and respect and would make his friend, Charles Clinton, his deadly enemy.

An explosion shook the railings of the garden and made the horses stir restlessly. 'It's begun again,' said John, and made sure that the shutters were fast across the windows in the rooms above the kitchen.

'How long do you think they will attack the Close for?' asked Jerard.

'For longer than it took the Roundheads to take it. They learned from their enemies that they must take in provisions and arms enough to last a seige,' replied John. 'It'll take time to shift them.' He finished his bread and drained the mug of ale. 'Come out at the back. It's not as noisy there. We can put up a target and have some practice, and I can sit on that great horse of yours.'

Jerard laughed. 'You take no heed of the fighting my friend? It is as if it is in another county!'

'They will fight or not, it makes no difference in the long run. Cromwell is strong and the people are tired of debt and taxes, but the King has no witch hunts and is liked by all who enjoy life, so you take your choice.' He shrugged. 'I make no

126

choice but to work and give my children a roof under which to live in peace.'

'You make it sound simple,' murmured Jerard. 'I came to ask if I may stay here for a day or so until the fighting ends. I have to send word to Sir Edwin to tell him of what is happening here, and I have as safe a passage as any diplomat. They see my hat and know that I am a foreign fool who is harmless.' He laughed.

He took out the shining crossbow and secured a bolt. John set up a bale of straw and a wooden block on it, eyeing the weapon with respect. 'That is no toy for a fool,' he said, and watched the sharp impact as the silent bolt took the block from the straw at fifty paces. 'I see that you are no longer king of the crossbow. You wear only the pin with the handgun. Was my repair so bad that you leave it at home?'

'I left it in good hands. I hate to think of losing it again. It is secure and will, I think, be well protected from any who might want to steal it. If I die, it shall rest where it is,' he said simply.

'So you admit that death comes to all?' said John. He laughed. 'The grooms have come for the horses. I will see them go, and then come back here. We can go into the woods on this side of the city where we shall hear no guns and maybe rope a deer. I am allowed to take three in payment for my work for the General, but it isn't wise to shoot as we may be mistaken for soldiers and become targets ourselves.'

Jerard raised his crossbow. 'I will bring my friend,' he said, and watched John coil the bolas neatly on the pommel of his saddle.

They left the horses in a grassy clearing, hobbled but free to graze, until they found game, then John hurried back quietly and Jerard drove a small herd towards the clearing where John now waited with the weighted rope in his hands.

The first buck sniffed the air but smelled only horses, and the urgency of the does made him leave the shelter of the trees as Jerard beat the bushes behind them. John turned his horse slightly to have a better swing to the rope, and Jerard came into the clearing in time to see the weights hurl through the air and twist the rope round the hind legs of a fat buck, bringing it to the ground.

John slid from the saddle and ran to the fallen animal, dispatching it quickly with his knife before untangling the rope.

'Make me a rope like that, my friend and I will pay you well,' said Jerard, his face alight with admiration and eagerness to try to emulate the farrier.

John laughed. 'First you must practise on a tree or a post as it is harder than it looks.' He handed up the rope as soon as Jerard was mounted. 'Be careful. It may snake back and harm your mount.'

'Then I will practise on foot,' said Jerard. 'This horse is not mine, and it would anger Sir Edwin if harm befell him.'

'There is a post in the field behind the cottage. I want to go back as I never leave Lucy alone for long and we must see what is happening in the Close.' They slung the buck over John's saddle and walked the horses back to the field. 'I'll call you when dinner is ready,' shouted John, as Jerard, with an air of intense concentration, tried to master the seemingly simple weapon, with many oaths and a stubborn resolve to be as good as his tutor before the day was through.

'All quiet?' asked John as soon as he entered the kitchen.

'One of the grooms came back for a bridle, but I told him that you were out the back and he went off in a hurry.' Lucy laughed. 'There's no call for you to worry about me, my love. As your wife, they don't dare lay a finger on me, and even that one would be too frightened to try. You never leave me for long and do all your work here now, so they have to look further if they want a woman.' She opened the bread oven and thrust the wooden paddle in to fish out the loaves. 'I think he may have been after the bread and not me,' she said, smiling at John when she saw that he was angry. She tossed a hot bun to him and he tore it open, relishing the hot sweet dough.

'Your father used to come begging when my mother made these,' Lucy said, almost sadly. 'That was in the old days before he took against her and became besotted with Parliament.'

'He's still inside the Close with Francis Turner and the others. They were quick enough to go there to avoid trouble, but they must wish it was all over and they could walk free again,' said John. He washed a bucket and filled it with the umbles from the buck. 'Scald the liver and I'll take it to the families along the way,' he said. 'The flies won't get into it if the blood is gone, and they can eat it before it goes to maggots.'

'I'll stew some of the meat and put some in salt,' said Lucy. 'There's enough saltpetre to do the haunches when the venison has hung a while, and we can have the brains and sweetbreads today.'

John smiled. The sound of gunfire came intermittently as the barrage grew louder, and yet he sensed no personal menace to himself or his wife in the cottage kitchen. Lucy calmly planned the food for the next week and scrubbed the table ready for dinner before setting out the pewter mugs, wooden platters and spoons, as if it were an ordinary day in April when the only discordant sounds should have been the rooster crowing and the cow in the yard mooing for a lost calf, instead of the sharp crack of guns and the heavy explosions of grenados filled with gunpowder.

Jerard came to the table breathless but exultant. 'You shall see how I progress,' he boasted. 'Later tomorrow I shall sit on a horse and see how I manage the rope from a height. I no longer hit myself, so the stallion will be safe from me!'

'Let Lucy put balm on your bruises,' said John. He grinned. 'You must have bruises. All men have when they try that game, and many give up before they are skilled. I was taught by a man who had used the bolas in a country away across the sea where Spain has dominion. He carries one everywhere and enemies never think a rope is equal to the sword until they are entangled and helpless.'

'It is silent,' Jerard remarked with satisfaction. 'I shall use it when hunting and as a defence. It is as deadly as a snake, it leaves no lead in the carcass, and the hide is undamaged.'

'First, we must ride round to the back of the guns and see what is happening,' John suggested, and they took a wide sweep away to the east and north to come to the mound where the heavy guns were placed. The guards watching the roads and lanes knew John the farrier and had heard of the strangely clad Frenchman who was neither fish nor flesh in this war and so unworthy of notice except as a butt for laughter at the tilt of his hat and the almost feminine fastidious cut and cleanliness of his shirt.

The cathedral lay within her thick walls, brushing off the onslaught as far as the first glance could tell, but closer inspection showed damage to the stonework and a splintering of the heavy wooden defences even though no breach had been made or seemed possible. Broken ladders lay where they had been repulsed from the walls, and bodies floated on the murky water where men had been flung from scaling ropes and had perished in the moat. Shouts of defiance from the towers and returned shots made a band of Royalists scatter back to the commander who had ordered a sortie.

Horses were kept in the rear as the Cavaliers knew that they were useless and vulnerable in a siege, but the frightened whinnying of tethered nags within the Close echoed from the walls to the answering Royalist mounts and made John wonder how they would fare without exercise.

He frowned. 'I have heard tales of the desecration of the cathedral,' he told Jerard, 'but until now, I never believed that they were using the holy nave as a stables!'

'Come away, my friend, before you show your anger and draw fire to us. There are men with muskets on the roof over there who are interested in anything that moves. If I die, I hope it is with a weapon in my hand and not as prey to some stray bullet from a duck gun!' he advised him.

'I must stay for a night, if you give me leave,' Jerard asked. 'Wyatt has thrown his lot in with the Prince and can take back a message freely to the manor, but I must stay to report any sudden changes in the fortunes of either side, and to warn the Clintons if they are in danger of being invaded by unwelcome guests. If the walls are breached, I may need a fast horse!'

The cottage was snug at night. Jerard slept by the smouldering fire in the one room that stretched the length of the building. He gazed through the half-light at the simple, sparse furniture and at the rabbits and hams hanging from the beam over the chimney smoke, and lay awake envying the couple in the upper room by the hayloft who could take their fill of each other with joy and the blessing of the Church.

He tossed and turned and went out to the yard to relieve himself, then walked in the garden to ease his bruised muscles. He saw lights in a window far away, in the now dark and silent city. He had seen women outside that house when he had ventured to wander with John Levett into the city, and John had laughed and explained that they had suffered the whip and the ducking stool and might have been hanged but for the reversal of the Roundheads' fortunes.

They were the town whores who now recouped their fortunes with the men of the Prince's army, blatantly once more, having no need to lurk in dark corners with Puritans too frightened to accost a woman in public for fear of punishment.

His flesh hardened and he dowsed his head in cold water, then took a mug of ale back to his couch. Dirty women had repulsed him for as long as he could recall and the thought of carrying the pox to Hope sickened him. 'Marry, or burn and die,' Edwin had said, but it wasn't possible. He couldn't take her to France and tell his family of her parentage, with no proof that she had noble blood in her veins. He shrugged. Misalliance happened in the best of families. Many of his good friends had a bar sinister on their coats of arms and were none the worse for it. They lacked no respect from society for the bastardy of their ancestors.

It was as well to stay on this hard couch for a few nights if only to decide his own fate and to wonder if he would lose good friends if he took the girl as his mistress and if he'd lose his family if he married her.

# IX

Hope Levett touched the gold brooch that she had pinned, concealed, under the deep fichu of her gown. No other person had seen it since Jerard had left it on her pillow, and she knew that if anyone else saw it and knew that it belonged to Jerard Barill, tongues would wag and people would believe that he had left it there after a night of love. Who would believe that he had left it for her with a note vowing eternal love and devotion even though they had never embraced or exchanged passionate kisses?

Each day seemed longer than the one before, as a week passed with no word from Lichfield other than what was brought by Wyatt or one of the other men. Of Jerard there was no sign, and she began to doubt his love as a fantasy in the mind of a man bent on seduction, while he was half drunk and had lost all respect for his host and his family.

She tried not to think of him creeping along to her room in the night, but the proof lay heavy and precious at her breast, hers until he claimed it again or hers for all time if he was killed. His plea that she might run away with him and live in France had at first filled her with a joy so deep that she had been forced to pretend to be ill in order to avoid the curiosity of Lady Hester, who would have taken one look at her radiant face and suspected the worst, but later she had thought more clearly and remembered her own mother's disgrace.

Is it better to live with the man whom I shall love for the rest of my life and perhaps lose him later to a more suitable marriage arranged by his family, or to take a husband chosen for me and live in peace and respectability in the familar surroundings of my childhood? she asked herself for the hundredth time. Away from him she was strong, but he had only to smile and kiss her hand again and she would weaken.

From the window she saw the man who had supped with them the night before. He rode easily and held the reins in hands that were finely fashioned and strong. Lady Hester had pleaded a migraine and left the table before the meal was finished, asking Hope to help her undress, so apart from a brief handshake and a quick glance at the dark blue eyes and still richly waved hair, she had taken no real notice of the new guest.

'He is French,' Lady Hester had said in a voice that brooked no questions and showed a sudden distaste for all that was foreign in spite of her affection for Jerard. 'Stay and read to me, and leave the others to talk. I am sick of talk about the war and I am uneasy to have that man under our roof because he rides with the Prince and makes us seem his allies.' She flung down her peignoir. 'Not that one, girl! The blue one.'

'I am sorry, my lady,' Hope said, reverting to her role as servant and wondering what she had done to deserve such an outburst.

'No, my dear, *I'm* sorry. It's just that I hate to have that man

136

here. He came once and did great harm, and now he comes as if nothing happened all those years ago, and Edwin seems to accept what he did as trivial.'

'Did he kill a man?' Hope asked in a hushed voice.

'Just the opposite!' Hester laughed but the sound was harsh and false. 'He brought life, but ruined a life in doing so, and then went away as if he had better things to do than clear up his own ordure.'

Hope turned pale. 'My mother?'

Hester nodded. 'You must know now or the servants will tell you, or talk behind your back. They have but to look at you both to see whose blood you bear, and the older ones remember him here with your mother.'

'My fa— . . . Sam Levett swore that he would kill whoever it was who sired me,' Hope said. 'As a child, I took little notice of what he said because he called many people "whoremonger", "thief" or "charlatan", and it was just his temper boiling out, but I remember *that* very well.' She looked up into Hester's face while she untied the ribbons on the silken slippers. 'Tell me his name.'

'Le Marquis Victor Dusquesne,' Hester said. Gently, she raised the girl to her own level and sat her in a chair by her side. 'Your blood is greater than mine, Hope, and I now think that he never knew that you were conceived. God is just. He gave him no other issue from his wife, and so Dusquesne travels the world in search of adventure at an age when most men tend to their estates and their families.'

'Is he to be here for many days?' asked Hope. 'I will keep to my room if that is what you wish, Lady Hester.'

'I shall speak to my husband, and he will decide what to do.

I can never be discourteous to a guest, and to one who in the past was welcome here.'

Hope went to her own room but not before she had walked quietly along the gallery and peered down at the men seated there by the fire in the Great Hall. A dog growled softly and looked up into the darkness but sensed that whoever stood in the gallery was familiar, so he lay with his head on his paws, alert but not aggressive. Sir Edwin was listening politely to the Frenchman, and the other men talked among themselves, sitting apart from the head of the house and his guest.

'You are my father,' Hope whispered. She saw the rich fur edged jacket cast carelessly across a stool, the fine leather boots and the jewelled buttons on his shirt and remembered her mother, half-starved and dying in misery because of this man. As if aware of being watched, Victor Dusquesne glanced up at the gallery and then into the fire. There was nothing up there but darkness, and yet he had a sudden vision of a face he had almost forgotten. So many memories now flooded back of a summer when he had dallied here with the prettiest maid he had ever met, who had quite stolen his heart.

'When I was summoned home to see my father who was dying, I left this house with many regrets,' he said to Edwin with a shrug. 'Once there, life became too difficult for me to travel again for years, and I married the woman my father chose for me.'

'You were a welcome guest,' Edwin assured him. 'We were sorry to see you go.'

'Sitting here with you again, the years are gone.' Victor Dusquesne moved restlessly. 'I left something of my heart with you, Sir Edwin, and now it seems like yesterday when we

138

sat here and talked after riding your good horses and hunting. I feel that a part of me has never left England.'

Abigail put a full jug of wine on the table between the two men and caught her breath so sharply that Victor looked at her for the first time. She put a hand on the table to steady herself even though her head was clear of wine and she had all her senses.

'*Mon Dieu*! You were here before!' he said. 'Tell me what happened to the girl who was here as servant to Lady Hester?'

Abbie gave a coarse laugh. 'You did leave a little bit of yourself here, sir, that's for sure, but your little light of love is dead.' She picked up the other jug to refill it, and left the room.

Edwin sprang from his seat and then subsided, avoiding the puzzled and horrified glance of the Frenchman. 'Abigail has been with us for years and takes advantage of our familiarity.'

'But what she said, is it true? The girl died? She had a husband, I remember, but left him to work here where she was happy.'

'She went back to Lichfield,' Edwin said slowly, and wished that he had Hester by his side to help him now. 'She was ill and could not work after she was delivered so she went back to Quonians Lane. It was not our choice. Her husband demanded it.' As if a further explanation was necessary, he added, 'My wife wished to adopt the child, but it would have caused scandal as it might have been thought to be mine, so we left it and took the child into our service as soon as she was old enough.'

'And now what of the child? Is it with you?'

Edwin was startled by the sudden fire in the man's eyes. He paused, looking very serious. 'She is with us,' he said. 'She is also our ward now, and we have full responsibility for her. Her father dares not claim her again as witnesses would swear that he ill-treated her and attempted incest, but was prevented from doing so by Hope's brother.'

'You say her *father*? Then the child was not mine?' The fire died in his eyes. 'No, it was not possible. I have no heir, no child of my marriage, and so I travel and never find a happiness such that I enjoyed here for those few weeks so long ago.'

'The child *was* yours, Victor. Her mother refused to admit it to anyone, but there was no hiding it. She has your stamp on her and is far above any servant's issue. Abigail saw her in your face, and so will all who knew you and Hope's mother.'

'I must see her!'

'No,' said Edwin firmly. 'As her guardian I forbid it until she knows the truth and asks to see *you*. To her you are the villain who deserted her mother and left her to die of sorrow. Hope will think of you as the man who deprived her mother of joy and forsook his child, making it impossible for her to marry well.'

'She is my daughter!'

'Born in wedlock during her mother's marriage *to another man*,' Edwin reminded him. 'But surely of your blood, Victor.'

'I can give; I must give to her,' he began, and lapsed into speaking French so fast that Edwin had difficulty in understanding him.

'*Tais-toi*,' Edwin said at last. 'Be quiet and listen. You are as temperamental as my other guest, Jerard Barill, who is with the Cavaliers in Lichfield for a few days.'

'Barill is here? I know the family,' said Victor.

Sir Edwin regarded him with speculation. 'According to my

140

wife, he lusts after . . . your daughter, and she believes that his respect for our hospitality has worn thin. Is Hope to be an unhappy mistress like her mother? I can find a husband for her among my yeomen, but she is worth more.' He filled his glass and drank deeply. This was a night to share wine and confidences. He filled the empty glass by Victor's side.

'A yeoman? My daughter, the wife of a peasant?' His indignation was amusing.

'Half an hour ago, you had no idea that you had ever made a fruitful union with *any* woman, and now you speak as if you have brought this girl up as a princess,' Edwin pointed out. 'There is no call of the blood, is there? Is it not, rather, that you are proud to know you are not totally incapable of siring? Leave her with us, but also make provision for her to ensure a good marriage.'

'I shall go into Lichfield tomorrow and make changes in my Will. I shall leave monies in your care to administer for her, and I will not trouble you again, my dear friend.' His eyes brightened. 'Promise me one thing, though: when she has married well and has an heir, tell me and he can have his full inheritance. In France we have a better view of bastardy when it is once removed, and a male grandchild could be seen as an heir.'

'Tomorrow, I shall send her to one of the cottages with a message and you shall see her from the windows to prove that she is yours,' suggested Edwin. 'Go back to France and I promise to be scrupulous on her behalf. I will have a miniature painted of her so that you will know that she exists and you can show her likeness to your friends.'

Hope heard the men leave the hall, clattering up the

wooden stairs and shouting their goodnights, but no step paused by her door, and she heard nothing that was said in the room where Edwin Clinton now went to bed with his wife, and in the morning, she woke to the sounds of horses being made ready for the ride into Lichfield.

Before she had drunk the first ale, Hope was summoned to dress Lady Hester's hair and was told to take a package to the wife of the shepherd in the cottage on the far side of the farm-yard. Yawning, Hope walked slowly past the front windows of the manor, dreamily watching the birds dragging worms from the moist earth and listening to the robin that had bossed its territory for the last two years. She raised the hem of her skirt to avoid the dew, and the early morning sun made bronze lights glow in her luxuriant hair.

In the upper window, Victor Dusquesne watched the girl who mirrored her mother and yet had the same colour eyes and hair as his, the same firm chin and a nose that had its match in many of the portraits of Dusquesne ancestors. He sighed and turned away, full of regrets and a new sense of wonder, but he joined his men and when Hope came back, he had gone, out of her life before he had really entered it.

Lichfield was in a state of upheaval, with rumours making truth fiction and fiction truth. Dusquesne reined in his horse and his squire went ahead to find out what was happening. Men with scaling ladders stood ready to advance on the walls of the now unsteady defences, and the moat was empty of water but held instead a mass of bodies, killed in the first onslaught after miners had drained the moat of water by tunnelling beneath the walls from the north.

Cannonfire shook the walls and made a sorry sight as stone

and brickwork shattered. Men shouted in triumph as more and more mortars took a toll on the defences, and word spread that there was talk of a truce. Dusquesne found the lawyer whom Edwin Clinton had told him would see to his business with the greatest expedition, and stayed with him for two hours, making documents that would hold fast in any court of law and adding a codicil to his Will to be sent to France as soon as possible. He signed away a small fortune and felt shriven of any guilt he may have harboured for the girl whom he had seduced, and for her daughter, so much like his own self that he longed to claim her and take her back to France, but knew it to be impossible.

He ate with the lawyer and then watched the troops forming for another sortie against the Close defences. A flag of truce fluttered from the tower of the cathedral and a cry went up that the Roundheads were about to surrender. Men who had stayed away from the fighting, dressed soberly as they had done during the occupation of the Parliamentarians, now sported bright waistcoats and hose and came out to cheer. Food hidden in cellars was brought out to cook over open fires in the square and the Cavaliers were toasted as saviours.

John Levett watched, and smiled wryly. These same people had cheered the Roundheads when they had marched through the city, and would turn coats again if it suited them. He made Lucy stay out of sight, knowing the mood of victory and the passions of the soldiery. A thin line of men and women, held hostage during the siege, filed out of the Close and were greeted by their families. The firing had stopped and officers of the Royalist army rode up to the portcullis. John saw men who had shouted for Oliver Cromwell, dressed in the sober raiment of Puritans, emerging cautiously as citizens now free to mingle with their peers who had supported the Crown or gone about their daily work and sworn allegiance to neither side. These men from the Close slunk away, afraid of reprisals from their neighbours.

He saw Francis Turner and Sam Levett come out with heads down to avoid being recognized, and John grinned. People had long memories and would never let those two forget that they had been vociferous in denouncing innocent men and women for witchcraft and fornication.

They went directly to Quonians Lane, and John followed them in time to see them mount and ride away with bundles of clothes and provisions as if bound for another place. 'They've gone,' he told Lucy. 'I'm not sorry to know they'll not come back unless Oliver takes this city again.'

'They stole one of your nags, John,' said Lucy. 'I dared not say anything, and they took food from Meg Turner that she can ill afford to lose.'

'Take her some venison. We have plenty now, and take fish from the last catch I made in the night,' suggested John. 'With them gone, we can keep an eye on her. As for the horse, it was one I would have put down if it didn't recover from the scours. They took the first they saw that I had left apart from the rest in case they caught whatever ailed him. Jane Willow would have advised me, but she can come back and live here now all is safe, and bring her cures with her.'

'May we watch the Roundheads leave, if that is what will happen? Do you think they'll remain as prisoners, or be allowed to join their armies?' asked Lucy. She was excited. 'I can visit Hope again and feel safe along the road.'

'I'll take you,' said John. 'I shall ride with Jerard Barill to take the news to Sir Edwin and we can see Hope at the same time.'

'Today?' she asked.

'Tomorrow. We must make sure that the truce holds before we send word to Sir Edwin, and I must see what damage has been done to the cathedral.'

Women who had been afraid to visit the water pumps near the Close now threw away buckets of stale water and joined their cronies to gossip as they had done before the sieges. An air of optimism gathered force and hints of celebration came from the bolder spirits.

'We shall have the maypole again and the men's morris,' said one.

'I can wear my best dress and not be called a whore,' said a pretty girl who had been ducked for inciting lust among the soldiers. The men were more aggressive, remembering the spite of men like Sam Levett, and a search began, to root out sympathizers of Oliver Cromwell among the citizens.

By nightfall, the gaol in Lichfield House was empty of Royalists and yet bursting with so-called spies for Parliament, awaiting trial before the overworked courts.

Cavaliers approached the cathedral and paused to listen, but there was no sound within the graceful walls. All horses had been taken and all armaments had gone with the Parliamentarians, leaving the acrid smell of dung and urine in the choir and in the Lady Chapel. An air of forlorn shame hovered over the desecrated edifice, like a dignified old lady trying to hide the evidence of rape, and the men stood in horror, some secretly crossing themselves and others almost in tears.

Rage followed the grief as more and more evidence of delib-
erate damage was found; the beautiful stained glass windows
were shattered and the vestry vaults lay open, robbed of all the
church silver, and costly vestments lay torn in the mud. In the
darkness shouts of fear and anger filled alleyways as personal
scores were settled and more bodies were thrown secretly into
the muddy but drained moat, and at dawn, the solemn business of putting the Royalist dead into coffins and finding
space to bury them within the consecrated confines of holy
ground began.

A priest, who had spent the last two weeks in a cellar,
emerged as white as an earthed-up leek and brought out his
books to read services for the dead, fortified by good red wine
and freshly spitted venison, and messages went out to farms
to bring in food for sale if they had any left after the harsh
winnowing by Parliament men. Farmers whose land had been
left to rot while they were imprisoned, now went home to see
if wheat sown before the sieges had taken and might bear a
harvest, and horses and cattle that had been hidden in barns
were brought out to graze the spring bite and to fatten.

'We must give a full account of all we have seen,' said John
Levett. 'If I stay here, I shall do and say what I vowed I would
never do, take one side against the other. When the fire dies,
they will need men who are not biased to calm parish councils
and local business dealings, and I want only peace for all.' He
saddled his horse while Lucy watched and filled his saddlebag
with food and clothes in case he was delayed.

'I shall go with you,' Jerard insisted. 'I am afraid for the
good people at the manor now that the countryside is full of
wandering deserting soldiers and ex-prisoners.'

'I shall go to the Turners now that Francis has left,' said Lucy. 'They will look after me.' She smiled wanly. 'I send my love to Hope but the thought of riding a horse sickens me. Tell her that I am with child and she will not see me there until the sickness has passed.'

'You are fortunate, my friend,' said Jerard after half an hour of silent riding. 'You have good work and a place in the hearts of the people you know, you have a good and pretty wife, and now you will have an heir.' He laughed to hide his genuine emotion. 'And you can still handle that accursed rope better than I can.'

John grinned. 'I should have a badge of gold with entwined ropes to make me king of the bolas,' he announced, teasing.

'So you shall! As soon as I get back to the Rhône Valley, it shall be fashioned from the finest gold I can procure.'

'You go back soon?' John was serious. 'We shall miss you, but you must have many matters to attend to. You have been in England for a long time.'

'I must face what they have to offer me,' he muttered. 'It will not be easy.'

'What do you mean?'

'They expect me to marry, but I now know that I cannot. Your sister has put a spell on me and I can think of no other woman.'

'Lady Hester has made her a ward, and I have some say in what happens to Hope,' John reminded him. 'We shall look for a good marriage for her and guard her closely until she attains this.' His jaw set in a way that showed that he would brook no attempt to take Hope lightly. 'Any man who tries to take her

147

in lechery will have me to deal with. I would kill any man I found who threatened her in that way.'

He glanced sideways at the Frenchman. Jerard sat on his horse elegantly and his velvet cloak spread over the saddle and haunches of the black stallion in rich folds. The pride of ancient lineage showed in the set of his shoulders and the upturn of his chin, and the golden pin gleamed on his breast, but the blood that John had acquired through *le droit de seigneur* ousted all traces of Sam Levett as he regarded his friend sternly. 'Even you, Jerard, would have no mercy if harm befell my sister,' he said quietly.

John stopped by the edge of the spinney and they dismounted and let the horses crop while they took their food. 'What is that place?' asked Jerard. 'We have many such ruins in France, but that looks more like a fragment of a monastery than a village church.' He walked towards the ruined chapel and John followed him.

'We played here as children,' he said. 'It is a good hiding place and we found a loose stone that led to the crypt. It served me well when Jane Willow fled the Roundheads and I hid her here while they hunted her. I think that only very few people recall the hiding place now, and God willing we shall not have to use it again.'

He looked down at the trodden earth, where the imprint of heavy riding boots had made marks in the soft mud. Straw lay in heaps as he had once seen it, making a couch for at least two men, and he remembered that Francis Turner had used it when he was spying for Cromwell and had not dared show his face in Lichfield.

The stone that hid the steps down under the chapel was

covered as he had left it and he was glad to think that Francis had forgotten where he had once played. Perhaps he had never gone down into the crypt? John smiled. Francis had been afraid of the dark and of things that went bump in the night, so he may never have ventured below the stone, but John was oddly worried that someone had been sleeping there, so near to the manor.

Jerard brushed the grass from his breeches and they rode on to the manor and the Clintons.

Hope heard the horses and ran to the window. 'Is it Wyatt with news?' asked Lady Hester.

Hope instinctively put her hand to the outline of the brooch under her collar and gasped. 'It is my brother and Mister Barill,' she said, trying to hide her growing emotion.

'Send for wine and food, my dear. I shall receive them here and you shall speak to them, but later when they go to report to my husband you must attend your lesson.' She glanced at the ormolu timepiece on the mantel. 'Sir Edwin is with his steward but promised to be back soon.'

For the next half-hour, Hope sat demurely, but with a heart that threatened to burst, while John and Jerard told them of the Royalist victory and the terrible things they had found after the army had left under the flag of truce.

'You are better, Mistress Hope?' asked Jerard, but he had merely bowed when he saw her and made no attempt to take her hand. She was confused. Was this the manner of a man who had sworn eternal love and asked her to run off with him? She watched as he refused more wine and thought bitterly that he wanted to keep his head clear in case he made any more ill-considered remarks that might cause a girl to faint with love. He was false, she decided, and wanted only to take her as her mother had been taken, with little care for her future or wellbeing.

'I shall go to the priest and have my lesson, Lady Hester,' Hope suggested at last when she could bear the tension no longer. Jerard made as if to follow her, but Lady Hester engaged him in conversation so that he couldn't escape, and Hope ran down to the study where her books were laid out waiting for her and the priest sat reading a Greek text as if it were an easy news pamphlet. They sat by the window while Hope read her lesson and saw Sir Edwin return to the house.

Later, I must see Jerard, Hope vowed. He can't have forgotten everything he said in that note even if he was half-drunk at the time. She tried to concentrate on her lesson but was glad when the subject was changed and she could read French. Jerard might be proud of her progress, she thought to comfort herself. He could teach me more and we could ride and talk in his own language, and he might want me, for ever.

'You improve very fast, my dear,' said the priest benevolently. He glanced at the tray of wine and sweetmeats that Dorcas had left for him. 'I think we must not strain your mind any more. Come back in half an hour to study mathematics and I shall have a lesson prepared for you.'

Hope sat on a stone bench by the door and let the sun warm her face. Perhaps he would come this way soon and they could talk. It was very quiet now that the other guests had left, and even the stable lads were not shouting today. She thought of the man she now knew to be her father and felt sad. He might not know of her existence, or he might have been told but have no feelings for a child born of a lover who had no lasting claim to his affection or status.

The spring day was alive with bees and the music of birds but Hope heard nothing, nor did she see anything of the flowers and green leaves, soft against the grey walls. Jerard would not come to her, and she would have to spend her life with some awkward and ill-educated man who would give her respectability and many children. She sighed and stood up to go back to the study, then saw a stable boy coming towards her.

'What is it?' she asked.

'There's a man by the gate who asks for you, Mistress.' He looked impressed. 'He gave me a silver piece to find you and asks you to go softly, so that no man can see you go.'

'He gave you no note?' The boy shook his head. Hope glanced at the study window and saw the priest deep into his Greek again. It must be a message from Jerard. There was no other man likely to summon her so imperiously and with the confidence that she would come to him. She took a deep breath, and walked quickly over the dense camomile lawn, releasing the scent as her shoes crushed the tender plants. Impulsively, she picked some flowers from the border as she passed and clutched them where she held her shawl to give herself courage for the meeting. The small gate, by an overgrown path, was slightly open as if someone had forced it ajar after many months of resistance.

Hope smiled tenderly. It was the right place for a tryst, under a weeping willow and by the side of a hedge that would soon burst into an extravagance of fine rhododendrons. She heard a movement and pulled the gate towards her so that she could go through the gap.

Rough hands seized her and another was placed over her mouth. She struggled, and the long grass was threshed under her feet, but the two men were strong and carried her out to a waiting horse. Her mouth was stilled by a gag of foul-smelling cloth, and she was thrust over the saddle like a sack of corn while Sam Levett sprang up behind her.

'Now you be quiet and we'll not harm you,' he said. Hope could only try not to choke and she was frightened of falling from the horse, so she stayed still, too shocked to think until a bunch of leaves brushed her face sharply and slapped her into sanity.

They'll miss me, she decided, with a fervent wish to be rid of Sam Levett and the other man whom she hated, Francis Turner, who rode ahead to make sure they were unobserved. Hope wriggled slightly and found her kerchief in the pocket of her gown. She let it fall to the ground just as they went past a turning in the wood and she knew that the flowers she had picked had fallen as soon as she was flung over the horse. At last she spat out the gag, but knew it was useless to scream and the motion of the horse was making her feel sick as she lay on her stomach, head down.

'Where are you taking me?' she asked at last.

'Somewhere nice and quiet until the hue and cry dies down, and then you'll be a lucky girl.' Sam gave a harsh laugh. 'It'll be your wedding day, my love. I promised you to Francis Turner as his bride, and bride you shall be once you've come to your senses and said you'll marry him.'

'I'll never say yes,' Hope asserted, then screamed, as a heavy whip descended on her buttocks.

'Now, Francis won't want to see you marked, my dear, so be

sensible and know what I do for you is right before the law. I'm saving you from the life of a whore and the misery you caused your mother by being born.'

She was taken from the horse and into the ruined chapel. Hope looked about her and backed away from Francis Turner who eyed her with avid anticipation. 'NO!' she cried.

'Let her be, Francis,' said Sam when Francis seized her wrist and forced his mouth on hers in a wet and onion-reeking kiss. 'You'll do this properly before a magistrate when we get to Tamworth and after she's been tamed by a night or two in here without food. Now where did you say the stone was?'

'Through here. I used to come here as a child and had forgotten about it until Jane Willow disappeared, then I recalled it and knew that it must have been here where they hid her.' Francis laughed. 'Afraid of the dark? You can have water but nothing more, and after all this time I've no idea what must be down there waiting for you. I never went right down there myself but there's tombs and corpses and maybe things we should fear from the dead.'

'I thought you'd been down,' said Sam. He hesitated. 'We don't want a corpse on our hands.'

'Na; it will do. I raised the stone and it smells dry and I threw down a bundle of straw. Here, take this jar of water and get down there. The witch came out whole so a girl in her health can too.'

With surprising meekness, Hope stepped down into the dark crypt, hoping that the men wouldn't follow her. Jane had confided in Lady Hester and her about the wine and candles she had left there and the fact that there had been no rats or damp.

'Weren't you frightened that someone would raise the stone

and find you?' Lady Hester had asked.

'There is a back way,' Jane replied. 'It is hidden by nettles but leads away from the chapel.'

Hope listened for the sound of the men leaving. She heard stones and pieces of wood being piled over the entrance to the crypt and then the horses being ridden away and she groped for the candle and began to explore her prison.

# X

'If you please, sir,' said Dorcas, for the third time. The tutor looked up and his eyes focused on the maid as he put a finger to mark the place in the book from where he had been interrupted.

'What is it?' he asked testily. He glanced at the library clock and gasped. 'Oh my, I am late for dinner! Why didn't someone call me?'

'Lady Hester told me to fetch you and Miss Hope,' Dorcas replied. 'Where is she? I thought you were teaching her French and all the fancy things a *lady* needs.' Her tone was scathing. 'Fine lady *she'll* be, if she doesn't watch out. Meetings by the back gate to the paddock and rides with gentlemen don't make you a fine lady.'

'What can you mean, my girl? Keep a civil tongue in your head or I'll say something to your mistress.' He was annoyed to be found reading instead of doing his duty. He looked at the clock again. 'Where is Miss Hope?' he asked. 'She went out for half an hour while I prepared a lesson fo her. Mathematics it was, I think. It is now long past noon.' He gathered his cassock round him and went quickly to the hall where the rest of the household were already at dinner.

'So engrossed in studies that you lost track of time?' asked Lady Hester, smiling. This tutoring was proceeding well, and each day when she asked Hope how much she had learned, she was surprised and pleased to find the girl still enthusiastic and eager for knowledge. Her glance went past the priest to the empty doorway. 'Where is Mistress Hope? Study makes her hungry and she is usually here before I am.'

The priest coughed. 'I sent her away for half an hour while I prepared a lesson and time passed, my lady. She didn't come back and so I continued with my own studies.'

'Dorcas, send the kitchen maid to find her and say that she will have no pasty if she doesn't make haste. The men will eat it all!'

Dorcas smiled. 'I'll tell her, my lady, but I think she'll not find hers. Mistress Hope went out by the back gate hours ago to keep a tryst.'

'What do you, mean?' Lady Hester looked angry, and Jerard Barill seemed to freeze in his seat.

'It's true, my lady.' Dorcas was enjoying the discomposure she had generated, and the expression of disbelief and pain on the handsome Frenchman's face did not escape her notice.

'How do you know?' Sir Edwin looked stern. 'This is no time for lies, Dorcas.' He thought of Victor Dusquesne and for a fleeting moment wondered if he had returned and taken Hope away with him.

Dorcas tossed her head. 'The stable lad told me. She went to meet someone hours ago.'

'Why didn't you tell me?' Lady Hester sounded worried.

'I thought there was no call for that, my lady. It isn't as if she is gentry and has to be protected,' said Dorcas maliciously.

156

'Send for the boy!' Edwin commanded, and Dorcas ran to the stables wishing now that she had said less.

'He gave me a silver piece,' the boy said, as he stood in front of his master and felt that he was in trouble. 'I didn't know better, sir. He said he was her father but to say nothing to her about that. Just to tell her that a gennelman wanted to see her by the gate. There was two of 'em with horses.'

'Did he look like a father?' Jerard asked.

'He were old enough, sir,' the boy said, 'but no gennelman in my way of thinking.'

'Sam Levett!' John cried. 'Sam and Francis Turner have taken her!'

Jerard let out a long, slow breath of relief and his inner rage subsided, leaving him amazed at the depth of his feeling and the sharpness of his jealousy when he had thought of Hope eloping with a lover. 'Then we must ride to Lichfield,' he said firmly. 'Your ward must be brought back safely.'

'Not Lichfield,' John said with a frown. 'They were slinking out of the city the last time I saw them, with packs of clothes and food and all the money they could lay their hands on, including all that Turner's mother had saved. They knew better than to try to take what is my own, except for the nag, but some said they stole silver from the church and took that away, too.'

'Then where, my friend? Are they vicious men? Men who would take pleasure in torture? Why Mistress Hope? I will pay them, if that is what they want. I will go to them to fetch her and pay *anything*.' Jerard paused and his face was white with passion. 'And if they have harmed her, *alors*, I will kill them.'

'I think they intend Hope for Francis Turner, and they will make her wed him, not in Lichfield, nor in a church, but before a magistrate, perhaps in Tamworth which is in the hands of Parliament. From here, they dare not go north and Tamworth has a Puritan Governor.'

'Send men on fast horses,' demanded Jerard. 'With a prisoner they can move but slowly. I shall go with them.'

'Stay here, Jerard,' advised John. 'I feel that she is closer than Elton Manor, but we can send two men there to ask if any have passed that way today.' He shook his head. 'Our men are in the woods and along the Elton Road with the Royalists to make sure that Oliver's men don't come that way and try to take the City again. It may be hard-going, but across country they can be back within a few hours. We must wait and search closer to home.'

'You are right,' admitted Edwin Clinton. 'I'll have the barns and all the cottages searched in case someone is harbouring these vipers.'

'I shall stay and help to search,' John Levett asserted grimly. 'My Lucy is safe now, and she would want me to find my sister. Come with me, and keep your eyes open. They met her at the small gate which is seldom used, so we may see signs there.'

Men were sent to search the farms and outhouses, and Dorcas wished she had kept quiet. Far from making trouble for the girl, she had engendered a deep concern for her welfare, especially in the heart of the Frenchman. They might find her, and bring her back, safely instead of losing her forever, and the upstart chit would have even more favours given her. Dorcas boxed the ears of the stable lad to relieve her own feelings and told him he had no right to tell what he had seen, choosing to forget that it was actually *she* who had set the cat among the pigeons.

Jerard led his horse to the gate and John saw that his crossbow was slung over the saddlebag. His own rope and gun were also ready, and he prayed that he would not have to kill his own father. With mixed emotions he went to the gate and pushed it open far enough to let the horses through. Crushed grass sent up a smell of freshness and the promise of an early summer, but the two men were more intent on tracing where the trodden earth and bent grass took them.

'*Ma pauvre*,' murmured Jerard. 'You struggled here. I will kill them, *ma chère*. Look! She carried flowers and I think she believed she would meet me here.'

'She tried to tell us where they were taking her,' said John. They reached the bend in the lane and stopped where the way took them either to Lichfield or to Elford. 'Here!' John leaped from his horse and bent to pick up a white kerchief. 'They went towards Elford and Tamworth.' He frowned, and Jerard, who had spurred his horse to follow the track, looked back.

'We must ride fast!' Jerard shouted.

'No. Others have been sent along that road and will bring news from Elton Manor and the men watching the lanes. One of the nags was slow and sick, and with an added burden would not have gone much further. I think they are hiding and will go on at night. They know this country and will find shelter and food in one of the deserted farmhouses.'

'Mistress Hope is with them. Who knows what they may do to her?'

'Be calm. I think this farm might be the one,' said John. 'I see smoke from a fire and I know the farmer here was shot for resisting soldiers at Lichfield Market, and his wife fled to the safety of friends.'

They tethered the horses in a small grassy clearing and quietly approached the house. Pump water lay spilled on the stones and a bucket was wet from recent use. The soft tearing of grass told them where the horses were grazing, and a smell of cooked chicken came from the kitchen window. Other fowl pecked amongst the grit and a couple of goats watched from the hedgerow as the two men walked forward.

John peeped in through a gap in the shutters and saw Francis Turner and Sam Levett sitting over their food. He glanced as far as the gap would allow, but saw nothing to suggest that Hope was in the room.

'She'd like this,' Sam said, laughing as he held up a chicken leg. 'That girl has a healthy appetite and must be getting a bit peckish down there.'

'Let's pray that *all* her appetites are as hearty. All that tender young flesh,' Francis said with a leer, nibbling at the succulent meat. 'I'll make a meal of her once I get her to myself.'

'You'll say the words before a magistrate first,' Sam muttered. 'I could take her for myself as she's none of mine. Don't you forget that, Turner.'

'And don't you forget that I am a regular soldier in Cromwell's army, and if I point the finger at you as the father of a girl taken in as ward to a Royalist family, and with a son who sympathizes with the Crown, you'll not take *anyone* ever again!' Francis boasted. He pushed back his stool and buckled his belt.

'Where are you going?' Sam's voice was sharp with suspicion.

'Just out to find eggs before it's too dark to see,' he replied.

'You'll leave her be? We said to leave her for two days, or she won't do as she's told.' Sam stood up, too, and shrugged on his jacket.

'I ought to see that the stone's still there,' Francis said with a grin. 'Wouldn't like anyone to find her all alone there in the dark.'

'No!' Sam picked up his gun and faced his companion. 'My wife was made a whore by the girl's father, but I'll have none of that for her. I might point the finger at you as a fornicator, and complain that you abducted my daughter.' For a long moment, the two men stared at each other, as stiff-legged as two curs edging up for a fight, then they relaxed and sat down again. Sam filled the mugs with more ale and pushed one across the table.

'Another minute and we might have had one less to fight,' said Jerard in a whisper. 'Perhaps the good ale will solve our problems.' He stepped back so that he was sure he couldn't be heard in the room. 'She is in the cellar, I think. We must find a way in at the back.'

'Be careful, and think of what he said.' John tried to remember the exact words, but something eluded him.

'They said she was in the dark, down below,' said Jerard. 'Come, my friend, you are the Englishman and yet I understand better than you.'

John followed him silently to the back of the house where steps led down to the cellar and the door to the grain barn stood open on the ravaged store. No attempt had been made to lock anything. There was no need because the Roundheads had taken anything worth eating, except for the few chickens and goats that had escaped when the farm was attacked, and the pigs that now rooted in the spinney would turn wild in time like their kin, the wild boars.

'Not here,' Jerard whispered in disbelief. 'There must be other, more secure, hiding places that we cannot see.' They went from shed to shed, and from pigsty to empty stable, but found no trace of the abducted girl.

'Quiet!' John whispered. 'They are coming out.'

'We shall see where they lead us,' Jerard replied and John sensed his excitement. 'They trust each other as much as a fox trusts a pack of dogs, and stay together in great anger, I think.'

Sam was shouting and Francis was trying to calm him. 'No, I shall stay awake and see that you keep your part of the bargain. I take the silver and you take the girl, with enough to fit you out in Tamworth after you are wed.'

'She might die of fright there and what good will she be then to me or to any except as dog meat? I want her docile, but not witless!' Francis muttered. 'That is a fearsome place with ghosts of the dead, I shouldn't wonder.' He shivered, recalling his fear of the crypt when he had gazed down into the darkness, but never dared to venture down the steps to see the tombs and whatever horrors lurked there.

'You'll believe in the Church next,' Sam said sourly. 'You always were a coward, Turner, and a rank hypocrite.'

'She must be further away,' said Jerard. He looked across the fields but saw nothing but darkness in the woods, and the thin light of the stars hardly lessened the blackness.

'We know that they will lead us to her. If we stay close they must move soon, or fight again.'

'So, my friend, you sleep and I shall watch the stars and ask them to plan my future,' said Jerard.

'I shall watch,' said John firmly. 'She *is* my sister.'

'Go to sleep. You have your Lucy and your heir soon. I have neither, but a need to know that Hope is safe, and so I shall not sleep.'

He leaned back against a stone wall and pulled his cloak round him and five minutes later, John whispered to him but heard only light and regular breathing. He smiled. Such emotion was exhausting and he let the Frenchman sleep until the sky cleared of night and the first birds sang.

Francis Turner urinated in the yard and then drew fresh water from the pump. He yawned, and John suspected that both men had slept under the influence of the strong ale. Sam Levett followed him and then disappeared into the house after swilling his head under the pump. They ignored each other and Jerard, who had woken up refreshed, laughed softly. 'They make unpleasant bedfellows,' he whispered.

John eyed the pump with longing, his watch of many hours having made his eyes prick behind the lids, but he dared not go into the open yard. The bread in his pack was stale now, and dry in his mouth without something to wash it down with, but Jerard seemed not to be put out by the dew, the chill of the morning or the fact that they had eaten nothing substantial for hours.

'Until she is found, I shall not eat,' he said firmly. 'Today, they will lead me to her, and then I shall kill them.'

'Well, try to leave them alive until we know where Hope is hidden,' John said drily. 'We don't want *three* corpses.'

'*Mon Dieu!*' breathed Jerard. 'Let us go now and seize them by the throat and shake the truth from them.'

'Wait. She may be here in a hidden room. If they leave the farm, we can search the whole house and then follow if we don't find her, but if they stay we shall know she is still here.'

Sam Levett came out wearing his jacket, and his gun was in his belt. He made for the horses he had left by the orchard wall and saddled the best of the two. Francis Turner followed him and eyed the limp flanks of the other nag, which looked even worse in the morning light and hung its head down as if it had no strength left. Wordlessly, Francis saddled it and pulled at the bridle to make it walk, then elbowed Sam out of the way and mounted the better horse. Sam slowly followed him along the grassy track away from the lane.

John ran into the farmhouse and called softly while Jerard opened every door and peered into dim recesses, but the silence told them both that all life had left the house and that Hope was not there. 'They have taken everything,' John said. 'That means they are not returning here and will take Hope to Tamworth today.'

They saddled their horses and followed the two men easily, keeping a distance, well out of sight. 'They are going back the way they came,' John noticed. 'There is another farm about a mile away where they could have left her.'

'You were right to leave them alive for a little more time,' said Jerard. 'We might never find her unless they lead us there, or we force the truth out of them.'

'They can't go far with that nag,' said John. 'Three people on one horse will make Tamworth seem a long way off if that weak one falls, and if Hope is not as cowed as they think, she will be hard to keep still without a cart or horse on which she can be bound.'

'I know this place,' Jerard said suddenly. 'Over there is the ruin you showed me.'

'And I have been a fool,' John said bitterly. 'That's where they have hidden her. Francis Turner played there, as did we all as children, but I had forgotten that he knew the secret. Not that he ever ventured into the crypt, as he was a coward even then.'

The two men before them approached the meadow in front of the ruin and paused. 'Now?' whispered Jerard. 'I will take the younger one.'

'I can't kill my own father, even if I hate him,' John said, turning pale.

'Unseat him with your rope, my friend, and we shall have one with a ready tongue to tell us what we want to know, but the other will be mine. He has insulted the woman I love, and therefore my honour.'

Jerard drew a bolt from his pouch and fitted it to the crossbow. He nodded, and John swung the heavy rope round his head and let it snake through the air, bringing the horse down with a sickening crash.

Francis Turner swung round in the saddle and tried to reach, for his handgun, but his horse reared in fright when it heard the other nag fall, screaming. The polished bolt snicked through the air, and before he could even shout, he fell with the bolt through his heart.

Sam Levett fell into a blackberry patch, which broke his fall but did little for his comfort as the thorns dragged at his hands and legs when he attempted to get free. John quickly unwound his rope from the hind legs of the now silent horse and seeing that its leg was broken, put a gun to its head and put it out of its misery. He took the gun from the saddle and threw it out of reach of the man who now struggled from the briars, his hands bloody and his clothes torn and muddy.

'Where is she?' John's huge hands held his father firmly, and he shook him as if he were a small dog and not a fairly heavy man.

'It isn't what you think . . .' began Sam in desperation. He saw Francis lying on the ground, and the Frenchman cutting the bolt from his chest with as little emotion as he would have shown when flaying a deer for the pot. Jerard wiped the bloody bolt in the wet grass and dried it carefully on his handkerchief before placing it ready for use again.

'Two birds with one bolt?' Jerard suggested. 'It is right, *nest-ce pas*?'

'Tell me!' John shook Sam until his teeth rattled. 'I told you once before that I'd kill you if you ever laid a finger on Hope again, and by God, I'll do it if you don't lead us to her.'

'It was all proper. Francis was promised her, and they were to marry in Tamworth today. I wouldn't let him touch her until then, I swear in the Lord's name.'

'Which Lord? *Your* Lord, the Devil?' John said through gritted teeth. 'Don't waste time. Tell me. Is she in the old crypt?'

Sam nodded. 'Safe and with water,' he said hastily. 'I wouldn't have left her there, but I was afraid of what Francis might have done to her if she came with us.' It was a plea in an attempt to save his own skin. John relaxed his grip and Sam rubbed his sore shoulders, glancing apprehensively at Jerard who was turning out the pockets and saddlebags of the dead man.

'Interesting,' Jerard said, and the bright silver spilled out on to the grass. He undid the saddlebags on the dead horse and found more of the church silver filched from St Chad's, and the purse of money stolen from the Turner family. 'So you steal from your own kind as well as from Mother Church?' asked Jerard, with ominous calm. 'May I kill him now, my friend?'

'Let him go,' John said, turning to his father. 'Take the horse and get out, and never come back or I swear you will never live to see the three spires again.'

Sam stumbled in his haste to mount, and they watched him ride away, muddy and stained with his own blood but still venomous. 'My lord, Oliver, will be back!' he shouted, as soon as he thought he was safe. 'Then all foreigners will die on the gibbet. You murdered a good soldier, and I shall make you pay.'

John seized his gun and ran to the edge of the clearing. 'Come back, my friend,' said Jerard. 'We have more important matters to attend to. I shall have left England long before Cromwell ever comes to power again, and now your sister is waiting.'

John led the horses to the ruin and showed Jerard where the stone trapdoor lay hidden under the pile of wood and pebbles. There were more stones there than there had been when John last concealed the entrance, and he knew that this was to prevent Hope from pushing back the stone from below.

'Hope? *Mon cœur*, we come to you!' Jerard shouted, as he pulled away a large log and John used a plank to push aside the stones.

'I can hear nothing,' John said, with growing fear. 'Sam may have lied, but I can think of no other place where she might have been hidden, and we could see that they were coming here.' He worked on, cursing the dust which he blamed for the sudden moisture in his eyes. Memories of Hope as a child came to his mind, and thoughts of her laughing and carefree at the manor over the past few months made his heart heavy as the silence below seemed even more complete, as shattering as a blow.

Both men were dusty, and Jerard, who had flung down his velvet jacket when he came to free the stone, had streaks of mud on him where sweat mingled with the grime and stuck the silk to his body. His eyes were wild when at last the men pushed away the stone and peered into the blackness.

'Hope!' John shouted in a hoarse voice.

*'Mon Dieu! Elle est morte!'* Jerard ran down the narrow steps and into the crypt. In the slit of light coming through a crack at the back of the gloom, he saw a shape on the straw and stopped. 'Hope?' He whispered in French and English a mixture of endearments and entreaties, and sank to the floor when the bundle didn't stir. 'My friend, I am a coward. I cannot look. Tell me how she died.'

John bent down and pulled back the cloak that once had sheltered Jane Willow, and saw that there was no sleeping girl, no corpse under it. 'She's gone,' he said in a flat voice.

'Gone? Dead?'

'No, Hope isn't here.'

'They lied!' Jerard pulled at the cloak as if to shake out some sign. 'Where is she? She has never been here!'

'Yes, she was here,' said John. He held up the fichu that she had worn on the day she disappeared. 'She left this as a sign that she had been here in case she was taken away again. Hope knew that I had put Jane here, and that I would come to look for her here once we had searched the manor and the farms.'

'They took her away?'

'No, she escaped them, but who knows if she gained refuge with honest people? The woods are alive with deserters and worse.'

'She could never have lifted that stone, and it was covered as we found it, enough to make two men weary!'

John smiled briefly. 'Francis Turner knew of this place, but had never been down here because he was afraid of ghosts. He knew nothing of the door at the back.' John strode to the chink of light and pulled the door open wide. A sea of nettles with a path trodden through the middle showed them the way that Hope had taken. Jerard backed away and sucked his thumb. 'They are as terrible as a snake,' he said. 'I am not fond of these plants because they bring out lumps on my body.'

'We must go back to the manor,' John decided. 'She may have found her way back, but we can search along the way as we return.'

They rode to the back of the crypt where the nettles ended and saw traces of grass and broken twigs through a dense part of the thicket. 'She was trying to get back to the manor by means of woodland paths.' John dismounted and led his horse under the low branches of hazel and willow, and they walked as Hope must have walked, over grassy banks and vistas of wild flowers, seeing the crushed bluebell leaves and smelling the rank odour of the vixen. From time to time the under-growth stirred, only to startle a rabbit and, once, a young fawn, but today the animals were free from the gun or the snare as the men kept their eyes open only for signs of the girl they longed to see.

'She had to come on to the road here,' John said at last,

when they were within a mile of the manor. They mounted their horses and rode quickly, shouting for grooms as soon as they reached the stable yard.

'Mistress Hope?' Jerard asked the groom, but the man looked at him blankly. He ran into the house and seized the first maid he could find. 'Where is your master? Where are Sir Edwin and Lady Hester?' The girl pointed up towards the main staircase and backed away from the unkempt, dirty man who seemed to her quite mad. Jerard pounded up the stairs, making them ring under his boots and saw Jane Willow leaving a room with a pile of soiled linen.

'Jane, is Hope here?' asked John.

'My dear man, what a state you are in to be sure,' she said calmly. 'Of course she's here. She's been in her bed these last twenty hours or more and is quite worn out, the poor maid.'

'I must see her,' Jerard said eagerly, his eyes misting and his mouth losing all hardness.

Jane smiled. 'You won't like what you see, Master.' She eyed his torn and dirty clothes. 'And you ain't dressed for the ladies.'

She moved to one side and pointed to the room she had left. 'Don't excite her, the poor lamb,' she said, shaking her head as she went down to the linen room. 'I think the priest has left.' Those words were as careless as an after-thought.

'The priest? *Mon Dieu*, he gives the last rites!' Jerard whispered, and walked as quietly as his riding boots would allow into the bedroom.

He sank to his knees by the bed and Hope stirred sleepily. She pushed back the sheet and saw his horrified expression when her bare arms came into view. Her face, too, was covered with fiery red blotches and blisters from where she had fallen in the nettles in her desperation to escape from the crypt. Without the fichu, which she had left deliberately, and the cloak that she had left in her panic to escape, her arms, neck and face had all been exposed to the nettles. She had walked in great pain back to the manor where Jane had covered the stings with a distillation of bistort to reduce the fire and then applied a soothing cream made from the juice of house leeks and wax. Hope's eyes peeped out of swollen lids and her cheeks were bruised and sore.

'You are alive,' Jerard said, as if he had just realized that life was worth living. '*Chérie*, you must be well. I want to take you away with me.'

Hope smiled, slowly and painfully. 'Where have you been?' she asked. 'You are so dirty I hardly know you.'

'And you are ugly with blisters and redness,' he retorted softly. 'And more beautiful than the flowers.' His hand took hers and he kissed the swollen fingers as if they were bathed in priceless perfume and dressed with emeralds.

'You were concerned, sir?' Hope asked demurely.

'I saw the priest leaving and thought you were dead.'

'He feels it was his fault that I was taken,' Hope said. 'He comes every hour to see if I am better, and prays over me so much that I wonder if perhaps I *am* dead!'

'He shall earn his absolution,' Jerard spoke softly.

'What of Francis Turner?' she asked, with a return of her fear.

'I killed him,' said Jerard simply. 'Levett has gone to Tamworth and the Roundheads, and Lichfield is busy clearing up after them.' He glanced back at John who stood grinning

171

with a mixture of relief and amusement at the sight of his beautiful sister looking as though she had scarlet fever. 'We had mercy on your foster father but I find it hard to believe that your brother is a Levett. He can still throw that rope better than I can, and so I shall have to give him a badge as King of the Rope.' He laughed. 'He shall come and visit us and I shall challenge him when I have become proficient.'

'You are going away?' Hope sank back on to the pillow and the sore patches stood out even more against her sudden pallor.

'As soon as you are better,' Jerard replied firmly.

'It is better so,' John told her gently. 'You must turn your mind to marriage and children as Lucy and I have done. Lady Hester will look after you, and you have nothing to fear from my father.'

'So fast, my friend?' Jerard brushed his dusty hair back from his brow. 'I may not be dressed for this ceremony, but your sister looks not to have much to offer in return just now, either,' he said, laughing. 'We are two derelicts, and so deserve each other. Tell the priest that he must bring his book and chasuble and earn his keep. We shall be married the day after tomorrow, when your rash will have faded and I shall have bathed and be smelling more of the boudoir than of the sty.' He looked haughty. 'My family must accept this and we shall go there soon to make it known, so you must have no fear and trust me, *ma petite*.'

'You have to ask my brother and my guardians,' Hope said, but her eyes were bright and her whole body softened with love.

'Indeed you must,' said Lady Hester, who had been listening behind Jerard, with mock severity. 'There may be others more worthy who will ask for her. Hope now knows who sired her, and she will have a rare fortune as soon as she marries.'

Jerard looked confused. 'But we are in love, *n'est-ce pas*?' he asked Hope anxiously. He stood up, and became even more aware of his unkempt appearance. 'I wish to marry your ward, Madame. I, Jerard Barill, with lands and wealth enough for a prince.'

'And Hope is the natural daughter of the Marquis Victor Dusquesne, accepted as his blood, and her son will be heir to his wealth,' said Hester, enjoying the sudden deflation of his pride. She took his hand. 'Marry her, but remember that but for a formality, she is above us both.' She turned at the door. 'In six days' time, sir, not two. We have preparations to make and the gown to have ready, and I must become used to the idea of losing my ward.' She smiled. 'And I cannot allow you into the bedroom of a virgin about to be married within the week. Come and play to me, after you have changed your clothes and told my husband what you did last night.'

'Send Jane to me, Lady Hester,' begged Hope. 'The lotion smells badly, but it is doing good and so I must endure it to be whole before my wedding.'

Jerard kissed her hands. 'Forget that terrible place, forget the war, for I shall take you far away into the peace of the Rhône Valley, where I was born.'

'I must come back some day,' she said tremulously.

'When your country has lost its madness and is at peace again,' he said. 'There is much to do in England before your king can sit safely on his throne again in London, and you will be safer away from this place, but we shall visit Sir Edwin again and take your brother back with us to hunt in our forests.' He laughed. 'He must come to be installed as King of the Rope, and to tell my men how he uses it.'